Praise for
Finn Family Moomintroll
and the Moomin books

"Jansson's evocations of nature are powerfully succinct . . . This is a terrific book for reading aloud."
—*The Washington Post Book World*

"A lost treasure now rediscovered . . . A surrealist master-piece."
—Neil Gaiman

"Jansson was a genius of a very subtle kind. These simple stories resonate with profound and complex emotions that are like nothing else in literature for children or adults: intensely Nordic, and completely universal."
—Philip Pullman

"Tove Jansson is undoubtedly one of the greatest children's writers there has ever been. She has the extraordinary gift of writing books that are very clearly for children, but can also be enjoyed when the child, like me, is over sixty and can still find new pleasures with the insights that come from adulthood."
—Sir Terry Pratchett

Finn
Family
Moomintroll

Tove Jansson

Finn Family Moomintroll

Translated by Elizabeth Portch

SQUARE
FISH

FARRAR STRAUS GIROUX

NEW YORK

Imprints of Macmillan

FINN FAMILY MOOMINTROLL.
Text and illustrations copyright © 1948 by Tove Jansson.
English translation copyright © 1958 by Ernest Benn Ltd.
All rights reserved. Printed in the United States of America by
LSC, Harrisonburg, Virginia.
For information, address Square Fish, 175 Fifth Avenue, New York, NY 10010.

Square Fish and the Square Fish logo are trademarks of Macmillan and
are used by Farrar Straus Giroux under license from Macmillan.

Library of Congress catalog card number: 89-45395

ISBN 978-0-374-35031-4 (FSG hardcover)
10 9 8 7 6 5 4 3

ISBN 978-0-312-60889-7 (Square Fish paperback)
20 19 18 17 16 15 14 13

Originally published in Finland as *Trollkarlens hatt* by Holger Schildts Förlag
First published in the United States by Bobbs-Merrill Company, Inc., 1952,
under the title *The Happy Moomins*
Book designed by Elynn Cohen
First Square Fish Edition: April 2010
Square Fish logo designed by Filomena Tuosto

mackids.com

AR: 5.2 / F&P: S

Contents

MOOMIN GALLERY   ix

PREFACE   3

CHAPTER 1   7

In which Moomintroll, Snufkin, and Sniff find the Hobgoblin's Hat; how five small clouds unexpectedly appear, and how the Hemulen finds himself a new hobby.

CHAPTER 2   25

In which Moomintroll suffers an uncomfortable change and takes his revenge on the Ant-lion, and how Moomintroll and Snufkin go on a secret night expedition.

CHAPTER 3   44

In which the Muskrat has a terrible experience; how the Moomin family discover Hattifatteners' Island where the Hemulen has a narrow escape, and how they survive the great thunderstorm.

CHAPTER 4   68

In which owing to the Hattifatteners' night attack the Snork Maiden loses her hair, and in which the most remarkable discovery is made on Lonely Island.

CHAPTER 5   85

In which we hear of the Mameluke Hunt, and of how the Moominhouse is changed into a jungle.

CHAPTER 6   110

In which Thingumy and Bob, bringing a mysterious suitcase and followed by the Groke, come into the story, and in which the Snork leads a Court Case.

CHAPTER 7   125

Which is very long and describes Snufkin's departure and how the Contents of the mysterious suitcase were revealed; also how Moominmamma found her handbag and arranged a party to celebrate it, and finally how the Hobgoblin arrived in the Valley of the Moomins.

Tove Jansson and the Moomins   154

A Timeline Full of Fun Facts About the World of Moomin 156

Moomin Gallery

Here are some of the characters you may meet in this book

Moominmamma

The center of the family, highly moral but broad-minded.

Moominpappa

A storyteller and a dreamer, and very loyal to his family and friends.

Moomintroll

As gullible as he is enthusiastic, he is also naïve and extremely good-natured.

The Snork Maiden

Moomintroll's lady friend and very occupied with romantic fantasies.

Snufkin

A vagabond, a musician, and Moomintroll's best friend.

Sniff

An adopted friend of the family, his main interest is accruing riches such as gemstones.

The Groke

The terror of everyone, the unmentionable horror.

The Muskrat

Would-be philosopher, likes to be left in peace.

Thingumy and Bob

A mischievous pair, too fond of pea-shooters and such.

The Hemulen

Fanatic collector of stamps and plants.

Too-ticky

Her common sense often restores order in the valley.

Little My

The family's small, disrespectful, yet extremely positive friend.

Finn
Family
Moomintroll

Preface

O ne grey morning the first snow began to fall in the Valley of the Moomins. It fell softly and quietly, and in a few hours everything was white.

Moomintroll stood on his doorstep and watched the valley nestle beneath its winter blanket. "Tonight," he thought, "we shall settle down for our long winter's sleep." (All Moomintrolls go to sleep about November. This is a good idea, too, if you don't like the cold and the long winter darkness.) Shutting the door behind him, Moomintroll stole in to his mother and said:

"The snow has come!"

"I know," said Moominmamma. "I have already made up all your beds with the warmest blankets. You're to sleep in the little room under the eaves with Sniff."

"But Sniff snores so horribly," said Moomintroll. "Couldn't I sleep with Snufkin instead?"

"As you like, dear," said Moominmamma. "Sniff can sleep in the room that faces east."

So the Moomin family, their friends, and all their acquaintances began solemnly and with great ceremony to prepare for the long winter. Moominmamma laid the table for them on the verandah but they only had pine needles for supper. (It's important to have your tummy full of pine if you intend to sleep all the winter.) When the meal was over, and I'm afraid it didn't taste very nice, they all said goodnight to each other, rather more carefully than usual, and Moominmamma encouraged them to clean their teeth.

Then Moominpappa went round and shut all the doors and shutters and hung a mosquito net over the chandelier so that it wouldn't get dusty.

Then everyone crept into his bed and, making a cozy nest for himself, pulled his blanket over his ears and thought of something nice. But Moomintroll sighed a little and said:

"I'm afraid we shall waste an awful lot of time."

"Don't worry," answered Snufkin, "we shall have wonderful dreams, and when we wake up it'll be spring."

"Mm-m," mumbled Moomintroll sleepily, but he had already drifted away into a hazy dream world.

Outside the snow fell, thick and soft. It already covered the steps and hung heavily from the roofs and eaves. Soon Moominhouse would be nothing but a big, round snowball. The clocks stopped ticking one by one. Winter had come.

Chapter 1

*In which Moomintroll, Snufkin, and Sniff find
the Hobgoblin's Hat; how five small clouds
unexpectedly appear, and how the Hemulen
finds himself a new hobby.*

One spring morning at four o'clock the first
cuckoo arrived in the Valley of the Moomins.
He perched on the blue roof of Moominhouse and
cuckooed eight times—rather hoarsely to be sure,
for it was still a bit early in the spring.

Then he flew away to the east.

Moomintroll woke up and lay a long time looking
at the ceiling before he realized where he was. He
had slept a hundred nights and a hundred days, and

his dreams still thronged about his head trying to coax him back to sleep.

But as he was wriggling around trying to find a cozy new spot to sleep he caught sight of something that made him quite wide awake—Snufkin's bed was empty!

Moomintroll sat up. Yes, Snufkin's hat had gone, too. "Goodness gracious me!" he said, tiptoeing to the open window. Ah-ha, Snufkin had been using the rope ladder. Moomintroll scrambled over the window-sill and climbed cautiously down on his short legs. He could see Snufkin's footprints plainly in the wet earth, wandering here and there and rather difficult to follow, until suddenly they did a long jump and crossed over themselves. "He must have been very happy," decided Moomintroll. "He did a somersault here—that's clear enough."

Suddenly Moomintroll lifted his nose and listened. Far away Snufkin was playing his gayest song, "All small beasts should have bows in their tails." And Moomintroll began to run toward the music.

Down by the river he came upon Snufkin who was sitting on the bridge with his legs dangling over the water, his old hat pulled down over his ears.

"Hello," said Moomintroll sitting down beside him.

"Hello to you," said Snufkin, and went on playing.

The sun was up now and shone straight into their eyes, making them blink. They sat swinging their legs over the running water feeling happy and carefree.

They had had many strange adventures on this river and had brought home many new friends. Moomintroll's mother and father always welcomed all their friends in the same quiet way, just adding another bed and putting another leaf in the dining-room table. And so Moominhouse was rather full—a place where everyone did what they liked and seldom worried about tomorrow. Very often unexpected and disturbing things used to happen, but nobody ever had time to be bored, and that is always a good thing.

When Snufkin came to the last verse of his spring song he put his mouth-organ in his pocket and said:

"Is Sniff awake yet?"

"I don't think so," answered Moomintroll. "He always sleeps a week longer than the others."

"Then we must certainly wake him up," said Snufkin as he jumped down. "We must do something special today because it's going to be fine."

So Moomintroll made their secret signal under Sniff's window: three ordinary whistles first and then a long one through his paws, and it meant: "There's something doing." They heard Sniff stop snoring, but nothing moved up above.

"Once more," said Snufkin. And they signaled even louder than before.

Then the window banged up.

"I'm asleep," shouted a cross voice.

"Come on down and don't be angry," said Snufkin. "We're going to do something very special."

Then Sniff smoothed out his sleep-crinkled ears and clambered down the rope ladder. (I should perhaps mention that they had rope ladders under all the windows because it took so long to use the stairs.)

It certainly promised to be a fine day. Everywhere befuddled little creatures just woken from their long winter sleep poked about rediscovering old haunts, and busied themselves airing clothes, brushing out their moustaches and getting their houses ready for the spring.

Many were building new homes and I am afraid some were quarrelling. (You can wake up in a very bad temper after such a long sleep.)

The Spirits that haunted the trees sat combing their long hair, and on the north side of the tree trunks, baby mice dug tunnels amongst the snow-flakes.

"Happy Spring!" said an elderly Earthworm. "And how was the winter with you?"

"Very nice, thank you," said Moomintroll. "Did you sleep well, sir?"

"Fine," said the Worm. "Remember me to your father and mother."

So they walked on, talking to a lot of people in this way, but the higher up the hill they went the less people there were, and at last they only saw one or two mother mice sniffing around and spring-cleaning.

It was wet everywhere.

"Ugh—how nasty," said Moomintroll, picking his

way gingerly through the melting snow. "So much snow is never good for a Moomin. Mother said so." And he sneezed.

"Listen, Moomintroll," said Snufkin. "I have an idea. What about going to the top of the mountain and making a pile of stones to show that we were the first to get there?"

"Yes, let's," said Sniff, and set off at once so as to get there before the others.

When they reached the top the March wind gambolled around them, and the blue distance lay at their feet. To the west was the sea; to the east the river looped round the Lonely Mountains; to the north the great forest spread its green carpet, and to the south the smoke rose from Moomintroll's chimney, for Moominmamma was cooking the breakfast. But Sniff saw none of these things because on the top of the mountain lay a hat—a tall, black hat.

"Someone has been here before!" he said.

Moomintroll picked up the hat and looked at it. "It's a *rarey* hat," he said. "Perhaps it will fit you, Snufkin."

"No, no," said Snufkin, who loved his old green hat. "It's much too new."

"Perhaps father would like it," mused Moomintroll.

"Well, anyway we'll take it with us," said Sniff. "But now I want to go home—I'm dying for some breakfast, aren't you?"

"I should just say I am," said Snufkin.

And that was how they found the Hobgoblin's Hat and took it home with them, without guessing for one moment that this would cast a spell on the Valley of the Moomins, and that before long they would all see strange things . . .

When Moomintroll, Snufkin and Sniff went out onto the verandah the others had already had their breakfast and gone off in various directions. Moominpappa was alone reading the newspaper.

"Well, well! So you have woken up, too," he said. "Remarkably little in the paper today. A stream burst its dam and swamped a lot of ants. All saved. The first cuckoo arrived in the valley at four o'clock and then flew off to the east." (This is a good omen, but a cuckoo flying west is still better . . .)

"Look what we've found," interrupted Moomintroll, proudly. "A beautiful new top hat for you!"

Moominpappa put aside his paper and examined the hat very thoroughly. Then he put it on in front of the long mirror. It was rather too big for him—in fact it nearly covered his eyes, and the effect was very curious.

"Mother," screamed Moomintroll. "Come and look at Father."

Moominmamma opened the kitchen door and looked at him with amazement.

"How do I look?" asked Moominpappa.

"It's all right," said Moominmamma. "Yes, you look very handsome in it, but it's just a tiny bit too big."

"Is it better like this?" asked Moominpappa, pushing the hat on to the back of his head.

"Hm," said Moominmamma. "That's smart, too, but I almost think you look more dignified without a hat."

Moominpappa looked at himself in front, behind and from both sides, and then he put the hat on the table with a sigh.

"You're right," he said. "Some people look better without hats."

"Of course, dear," said Moominmamma, kindly. "Now eat up your eggs, children, you need feeding up after living on pine needles all the winter." And she disappeared into the kitchen again.

"But what shall we do with the hat?" asked Sniff. "It's such a fine one."

"Use it as a wastepaper basket," said Moominpappa, and thereupon he took himself upstairs to go on writing his life story. (The heavy volume about his stormy youth.)

Snufkin put the hat down on the floor between the table and the kitchen door. "Now you've got a new piece of furniture again," he said, grinning, for Snufkin could never understand why people liked to *have* things. He was quite happy wearing the old suit he had had since he was born (nobody knows when and where that happened), and the only possession he didn't give away was his mouth-organ.

"If you've finished breakfast we'll go and see how the Snorks are getting on," said Moomintroll. But before going out into the garden he threw his eggshell into the wastepaper basket, for he was (sometimes) a well brought up Moomin.

The dining room was now empty.

In the corner between the table and the kitchen door stood the Hobgoblin's Hat with the eggshell in the bottom. And then something really strange happened. The eggshell began to change its shape.

(This is what happens, you see. If something lies long enough in the Hobgoblin's Hat it begins to change into something quite different—what that will be you never know beforehand. It was lucky that the hat hadn't fitted Moominpappa because the-Protector-of-all-Small-Beasts knows what would have become of him if he had worn it a bit longer. As it was he only got a slight headache—and that was over after dinner.)

Meanwhile the eggshell had become soft and woolly, although it still stayed white, and after a time it filled the hat completely. Then five small clouds broke away from the brim of the hat, sailed out onto the verandah, thudded softly down the steps and hung there just above the ground. The hat was empty.

"Goodness gracious me," said Moomintroll.

"Is the house on fire?" asked the Snork Maiden, anxiously.

The clouds were hanging in front of them without moving or changing shape, as if they were waiting for something, and the Snork Maiden put out her paw very cautiously and patted the nearest one. "It feels like cotton-wool," she said, in a surprised voice. The others came nearer and felt it, too.

"Just like a little pillow," said Sniff.

Snufkin gave one of the clouds a gentle push. It floated on a bit and then stopped again.

"Whose are they?" asked Sniff. "How did they get onto the verandah?"

Moomintroll shook his head. "It's the queerest thing I've ever come across," he said. "Perhaps we ought to go in and fetch Mother."

"No, no," said the Snork Maiden. "We'll try them out ourselves," and she dragged a cloud onto the ground and smoothed it out with her paw. "So soft!" said the Snork Maiden, and the next minute she was rocking up and down on the cloud with loud giggles.

"Can I have one, too?" squealed Sniff jumping onto another cloud. "Hup-si-daisy!" But when he said "hup" the cloud rose and made an elegant little curve over the ground.

"Golly!" burst out Sniff. "It moved!"

Then they all threw themselves onto the clouds and shouted "Hup! Hup, hup-si-daisy." The clouds bounded wildly about until the Snork discovered how to steer them. By pressing a little with one foot you could turn the cloud. If you pressed with both feet it went forward, and if you rocked gently the cloud slowed up.

They had terrific fun, even floating up to the tree-tops and to the roof of Moominhouse.

Moomintroll hovered outside Moominpappa's window and shouted: "Cock-a-doodle-doo!" (He was so excited he couldn't think of anything more intelligent.)

Moominpappa dropped his memoir-pen and rushed to the window.

"Bless my tail!" he burst out. "Whatever next!"

"It will make a good chapter for your story," said Moomintroll, steering his cloud to the kitchen window where he shouted to his mother. But Moominmamma was in a great hurry and went on making rissoles. "What have you found now, dear?" she said. "Just be careful you don't fall down!"

But down in the garden the Snork Maiden and Snufkin had discovered a new game. They steered at each other at full speed and collided with a soft bump. Then the first to fall off had lost.

"Now we'll see!" cried Snufkin urging his cloud forward. But the Snork Maiden dodged cleverly to the side and then attacked him from underneath.

Snufkin's cloud capsized, and he fell on his head in the flowerbed and his hat fell over his eyes.

"Third round," squeaked Sniff, who was referee and was flying a bit above the others. "That's two: one! Ready, steady, go!"

"Shall we go on a little flying tour together?" Moomintroll asked the Snork Maiden.

"Certainly," she answered, steering her cloud up beside his. "Where shall we go?"

"Let's hunt up the Hemulen and surprise him," suggested Moomintroll.

They made a tour of the garden, but the Hemulen wasn't in any of his usual haunts.

"He can't have gone far," said the Snork Maiden. "Last time I saw him he was sorting his stamps."

"But that was six months ago," said Moomintroll.

"Oh, so it was," she agreed. "We've slept since then, haven't we?"

"Did you sleep well, by the way?" asked Moomintroll.

The Snork Maiden flew elegantly over a treetop and considered a little before answering. "I had an awful dream," she said at last. "About a nasty man in a high, black hat who grinned at me."

"How funny," said Moomintroll. "I had exactly the same dream. Had he got white gloves on, too?"

The Snork Maiden nodded, and slowly gliding through the forest they pondered this awhile. Suddenly they caught sight of the Hemulen, who was wandering along with his hands behind his back and his eyes on the ground. Moomintroll and the Snork Maiden made perfect three-point landings on either side of him and called out brightly: "Good morning!"

"Ouch! Oh!" gasped the Hemulen. "How you frightened me! You shouldn't jump at me suddenly like that."

"Oh, sorry," said the Snork Maiden. "Look what we're riding on."

"That's most extraordinary," said the Hemulen. "But I'm so used to your doing extraordinary things that nothing surprises me. Besides I'm feeling melancholy just now."

"Why is that?" asked the Snork Maiden sympathetically. "On such a fine day, too."

"You wouldn't understand anyway," said the Hemulen shaking his head.

"We'll try," said Moomintroll. "Have you lost a rare stamp again?"

"On the contrary," answered the Hemulen, gloomily. "I have them all: every single one. My stamp collection is complete. There is nothing missing."

"Well, isn't that nice?" said the Snork Maiden, encouragingly.

"I said you'd never understand me, didn't I?" moaned the Hemulen.

Moomintroll looked anxiously at the Snork Maiden and they drew back their clouds a little out of consideration for the Hemulen's sorrow. He wandered on and they waited respectfully for him to unburden his soul.

At last he burst out:

"How hopeless it all is!" And after another pause he added, "What's the use? You can have my stamp collection for the next paper chase."

"But Hemulen!" said the Snork Maiden, horrified, "that would be awful! Your stamp collection is the finest in the world!"

"That's just it," said the Hemulen in despair. "It's finished. There isn't a stamp, or an error that I haven't collected. Not one. What shall I do now?"

"I think I'm beginning to understand," said Moomintroll slowly. "You aren't a collector anymore, you're only an owner, and that isn't nearly so much fun."

"No," said the heartbroken Hemulen, "not nearly." He stopped and turned his puckered-up face toward them.

"Dear Hemulen," said the Snork Maiden, taking him gently by the hand, "I have an idea. What about your collecting something different—something quite new?"

"That's an idea," admitted the Hemulen, but he continued to look worried because he thought he oughtn't to look happy after such a big sorrow.

"Butterflies for example?" suggested Moomintroll.

"Impossible," said the Hemulen and became gloomy again. "One of my second cousins collects them, and I can't stand him."

"Film stars then?" said the Snork Maiden.

The Hemulen only sniffed.

"Ornaments?" Moomintroll said hopefully. "They're never finished."

But the Hemulen pooh-poohed that too.

"Well, then I really don't know," said the Snork Maiden.

"We'll think of something for you," said Moomintroll, consolingly. "Mother's sure to know. By the way, have you seen the Muskrat?"

"He's still asleep," the Hemulen answered sadly. "He says that it's unnecessary to get up so early, and I think he's right." And with that he continued his lonely wanderings, while Moomintroll and the Snork Maiden steered their clouds right up over the tree-tops and rested there, rocking slowly in the sunshine. They considered the problem of the Hemulen's new collection.

"What about shells?" the Snork Maiden proposed.

"Or rarey buttons," said Moomintroll.

But the warmth made them sleepy and didn't encourage thinking, so they lay on their backs on the clouds and looked up at the spring sky where the larks were singing.

And suddenly they caught sight of the first butterfly. (As everyone knows, if the first butterfly you see is yellow the summer will be a happy one. If it is white then you will just have a quiet summer. Black and brown butterflies should never be talked about—they are much too sad.)

But this butterfly was golden.

"What can that mean?" said Moomintroll. "I've never seen a golden butterfly before."

"Gold is even better than yellow," said the Snork Maiden. "You wait and see!"

When they got home to dinner they met the Hemulen on the steps. He was beaming with happiness.

"Well?" said Moomintroll. "What is it?"

"Nature study!" shouted the Hemulen. "I shall botanize. The Snork thought of it. I shall collect the world's finest herbarium!" And the Hemulen spread out his skirt* to show them his first find. Among the earth and leaves lay a very small spring-onion.

"*Gagea lutea*," said the Hemulen proudly. "Number one in the collection. A perfect specimen." And he went in and dumped the whole lot on the dining table.

"Put it in the corner, Hemul dear," said Moominmamma, "because I want to put the soup there. Is everybody in? Is the Muskrat still sleeping?"

"Like a pig," said Sniff.

"Have you had a good time today?" asked Moominmamma when she had filled all the plates.

"Wonderful," cried the whole family.

---

*The Hemulen always wore a dress that he had inherited from his aunt. I believe all Hemulens wear dresses. It seems strange, but there you are. *Author.*

Next morning when Moomintroll went to the wood-shed to let out the clouds they had all disappeared; every one of them. And nobody imagined that it had anything to do with the eggshell which was once again lying in the Hobgoblin's Hat.

Chapter 2

*In which Moomintroll suffers an uncomfortable
change and takes his revenge on the Ant-lion[*],
and how Moomintroll and Snufkin go on a
secret night expedition.*

O ne warm summer day it was raining softly in the
Valley of the Moomins, so they all decided to
play hide-and-seek indoors. Sniff stood in the corner
with his nose in his paws and counted up to ten

---

[*]In case you don't know, an Ant-lion is a crafty insect who digs himself
down into the sand leaving a small round hole above him. Into this
hole unsuspecting little animals fall and then get caught by the Ant-
lion, who pops up from the bottom of the hole and devours them.
    You can read all about it in the Encyclopaedia if you don't believe
me. *Translator.*

before he turned around and began hunting—first in the ordinary hiding places and then in the extraordinary ones.

Moomintroll lay under the verandah table feeling rather worried—it wasn't a good place. Sniff would be sure to lift the tablecloth, and there he would be stuck. He looked about, and then caught sight of the tall, black hat which stood in a corner. That would be a brilliant idea! Sniff would never think of looking under the hat. Moomintroll stole quietly to the corner and pulled the hat over his head. It didn't reach further than his middle, but if he made himself very small and tucked in his tail he would be quite invisible. He giggled to himself when he heard all the others being found, one after another. The Hemulen had obviously hidden himself under the sofa again—he could never find a better place. And now they were all running about searching for Moomintroll.

He waited until he was afraid they would get bored with the search, and then he crept out of the hat, stuck his head through the door and said: "Look at me!"

Sniff stared at him for a long time, then he said rather unkindly, "Look at yourself!"

"Who's that?" whispered the Snork, but the others only shook their heads and continued to stare at Moomintroll.

Poor little chap! He had been turned into a very strange animal indeed under the Hobgoblin's Hat.

All his fat parts had become thin, and everything that was small had grown big. And the strangest thing about it was that he himself didn't realize what was the matter.

"I thought I'd surprise you all," he said taking an uncertain step forward on his long, spindly legs. "You've no idea where I've been!"

"It doesn't interest us," said the Snork, "but you're certainly ugly enough to surprise anybody."

"You are unkind," said Moomintroll sadly. "I suppose you got tired of hunting. What shall we do now?"

"First of all perhaps you should introduce yourself," said the Snork Maiden, stiffly. "We don't know who you are, do we?"

Moomintroll looked at her incredulously, but then it dawned on him that perhaps this was a new game. He laughed delightedly and said: "I'm the King of California!"

"And I'm the Snork Maiden," said the Snork Maiden. "This is my brother."

"I'm called Sniff," said Sniff.

"I'm Snufkin," said Snufkin.

"Oh, dear! How boring you all are," said Moomintroll. "Couldn't you have thought of something more original! Now let's go out—I think the weather's clearing." And he went down the steps into the garden, followed by a rather surprised and suspicious little trio.

"Who's that?" asked the Hemulen, who was sitting

in front of the house counting the stamens of a sun-flower.

"It's the King of California, I think," said the Snork Maiden.

"Is he going to live here?" asked the Hemulen.

"That's for Moomintroll to decide," said Sniff. "I wonder where he's got to."

Moomintroll laughed. "You really are quite funny at times," he said. "Shall we go and look for Moomintroll?"

"Do you know him?" asked Snufkin.

"Ye-es," said Moomintroll. "Rather well as a matter of fact." He was thoroughly enjoying the new game and thought he was doing rather well at it.

"How did you come to know him?" asked the Snork Maiden. "We were born at the same time," said Moomintroll, still bursting with laughter. "But he's an impossible fellow, you know! You simply can't have him in the house!"

"How dare you talk about Moomintroll like that!" said the Snork Maiden, fiercely. "He's the best Moomin in the world, and we think a great deal of him."

This was almost too much for Moomintroll. "Really?" he said. "Personally I think he's an absolute pest."

Then the Snork Maiden began to cry.

"Go away!" said the Snork to Moomintroll. "Otherwise we shall have to sit on your head."

"All right, all right," Moomintroll said, soothingly.

"It's only a game, isn't it? I'm awfully glad you think so much of me."

"But we *don't*," screamed Sniff, shrilly. "Take away this ugly king who runs down our Moomintroll."

And they threw themselves onto poor Moomintroll. He was much too surprised to defend himself, and when he began to get angry it was too late. So when Moominmamma came out on the steps he was lying underneath a large pile of flailing paws and tails.

"What are you doing there, children?" she cried. "Stop fighting at once!"

"They're walloping the King of California," sniffed the Snork Maiden. "And it serves him right."

Moomintroll crawled out of the scrum, tired out and angry.

"Mother," he cried. "They started it. Three against one! It's not fair!"

"I quite agree," said Moominmamma seriously. "However, I expect you had teased them. But who are you, my little beast?"

"Oh, please stop this awful game," wailed Moomintroll. "It isn't funny anymore. I am Moomintroll, and you are my mother. And that's that!"

"*You* aren't Moomintroll," said the Snork Maiden, scornfully. "He has beautiful little ears, but yours look like kettle holders!"

Moomintroll felt quite confused and took hold of a pair of enormous crinkly ears. "But I *am* Moomintroll!" he burst out in despair. "Don't you believe me?"

"Moomintroll has a nice little tail, just about the right size, but yours is like a chimney sweep's brush," said the Snork.

And, oh, dear, it was true! Moomintroll felt behind him with a trembling paw.

"Your eyes are like soup plates," said Sniff. "Moomintroll's are small and kind!"

"Yes, exactly," Snufkin agreed.

"You are an impostor!" decided the Hemulen.

"Isn't there anyone who believes me?" Moomintroll pleaded. "Look carefully at me, Mother. You must know your own Moomintroll."

Moominmamma looked carefully. She looked into his frightened eyes for a very long time, and then she said quietly: "Yes, you are my Moomintroll."

And at the same moment he began to change. His ears, eyes and tail began to shrink, and his nose and tummy grew, until at last he was his old self again.

"It's all right now, my dear," said Moominmamma. "You see, I shall always know you whatever happens."

A little later on, Moomintroll and the Snork were sitting in one of their secret hiding places—the one under the jasmine bush which was hidden by a curtain of green leaves.

"Yes, but you *must* have done something to change you," the Snork was saying.

Moomintroll shook his head. "I didn't notice

anything unusual," he said. "And I didn't say any dangerous words either."

"But perhaps you stepped into a fairy ring," suggested the Snork.

"Not that I know of," said Moomintroll. "I sat the whole time under that black hat that we use as a wastepaper basket."

"In the *hat*?" asked the Snork, suspiciously.

Moomintroll nodded, and they both thought for a long time. Then suddenly they burst out together: "It must be . . . !" and stared at each other.

"Come on!" said the Snork.

They went onto the verandah and crept up to the hat very cautiously.

"It looks rather ordinary," said the Snork. "Unless you consider that a top hat is always somewhat extraordinary, of course."

"But how can we find out if it *was* that?" asked Moomintroll. "*I'm* not going to get into it again!"

"Perhaps we could lure somebody else into it," suggested the Snork.

"But that would be a low-down trick," said Moomintroll. "How should we know that he would be all right again?"

"What about an enemy?" suggested the Snork.

"Hm," said Moomintroll. "Do you know of one?"

"The Pig-Swine," said the Snork.

Moomintroll shook his head. "He's too big."

"Well, the Ant-lion then?" the Snork suggested.

"That's a good idea," Moomintroll agreed. "He once pulled my mother down into a hole and sprayed sand into her eyes."

So they set out to look for the Ant-lion, and took a big jar with them. You should look for ant-lions' holes in a sandy place, so they wandered down to the beach, and it wasn't long before the Snork discovered a big, round hole and signaled eagerly to Moomintroll.

"Here he is!" whispered the Snork. "But how shall we lure him into the jar?"

"Leave it to me," whispered Moomintroll. He took the jar and buried it in the sand a little distance away, with the opening on top. Then he said loudly, "They are very weak creatures these ant-lions!" He signed to the Snork and they both looked expectantly down at the hole, but although the sand moved a bit nothing was to be seen.

"*Very* weak," repeated Moomintroll. "It takes several hours for them to dig themselves down into the sand, you know!"

"Yes, but—," said the Snork, doubtfully.

"It does I tell you," said Moomintroll, making frantic signs with his ears. "Several hours!"

At that moment a threatening head with staring eyes popped up from the hole in the sand.

"Did you say weak?" hissed the Ant-lion. "I can dig myself down in exactly three seconds!"

"You should really show us how it's done, so that

we can believe such a wonderful feat is possible," said Moomintroll, persuasively.

"I shall spray sand on you," replied the Ant-lion very crossly, "and when I have sprayed you down into my hole I shall gobble you up!"

"Oh, no," pleaded the Snork. "Couldn't you show us how to dig down backwards in three seconds instead?"

"Do it up here so that we can see better how it's done," said Moomintroll, and pointed to the spot where the jar was buried.

"Do you think I am going to bother myself with showing tricks to babies?" said the Ant-lion, huffily. But all the same he simply could not resist the temptation to show them how strong and quick he was, so, with scornful sniffings, he scrambled up out of his hole and asked haughtily:

"Now, where shall I dig myself in?"

"There," said Moomintroll pointing.

The Ant-lion drew up his shoulders and raised his mane in a terrifying manner.

"Out of my way!" he cried. "Now I'm going

underground, but when I come back I shall gobble you up! One, two, three!" And he backed down into the sand like a whirling propeller, right into the jar which was hidden under him. It certainly did only take three seconds, or perhaps two and a half, because he was so awfully angry.

"Quick with the lid," cried Moomintroll, and scraping away the sand they screwed it on very tightly. Then they both heaved up the jar and began to roll it home, with the Ant-lion inside screaming and cursing and choking with sand.

"It's frightful how angry he is," said the Snork. "I daren't think what will happen when he comes out!"

"He won't come out now," said Moomintroll, quietly, "and when he does I hope he will be changed into something horrible."

When they arrived at Moominhouse, Moomintroll summoned everyone with three long whistles. (Which means: Something quite extraordinary has happened.)

The others arrived from all directions and collected round the jar with the screw-top.

"What have you got there?" asked Sniff.

"An ant-lion," said Moomintroll, proudly. "A genuine furiously angry ant-lion that we have taken prisoner!"

"Fancy you daring!" said the Snork Maiden, admiringly.

"And now I think we'll pour him into the hat," said the Snork.

"So that he will be changed like I was," said Moomintroll.

"Will somebody please tell me what all this is about?" the Hemulen asked plaintively.

"It was because I hid in that hat that I was changed," explained Moomintroll. "We've worked it out. And now we're going to make sure by seeing if the Ant-lion will turn into something else as well."

"B-but he could turn into absolutely anything!" squeaked Sniff. "He could turn into something still more dangerous than an ant-lion and gobble us all up in a minute." They stood in terrified silence looking at the pot and listening to the muffled sounds coming from inside.

"Oh!" said the Snork Maiden, turning rather pale[*], but Snufkin suggested they should all hide under the table while the change took place, and put a big book on top of the hat. "You must always take risks when experimenting," he said. "Tip him in now at once."

Sniff scrambled under the table while Moomintroll, Snufkin and the Hemulen held the jar over the Hobgoblin's Hat, and the Snork gingerly unscrewed the lid. In a cloud of sand the Ant-lion tumbled out, and, quick as lightning, the Snork popped a Dictionary of Outlandish Words on top. Then they all dived under the table and waited.

At first nothing happened.

---

[*]Snorks often turn pale when emotionally upset. *Author.*

They peeped out from under the tablecloth, getting more and more agitated. Still there was no change.

"It was all rot," said Sniff, but at that moment the big dictionary began to crinkle up, and in his excitement, Sniff bit the Hemulen's thumb thinking it was his own.

Now the dictionary was curling up more and more. The pages began to look like withered leaves, and between them the Outlandish Words came out and began crawling around on the floor.

"Goodness, gracious me," said Moomintroll.

But there was more to come. Water began to drip from the brim of the hat and then to overflow and to splash down onto the carpet so that the Words had to climb up the walls to save themselves.

"The Ant-lion has only turned into water," said Snufkin in disappointment.

"I think it's the sand," whispered the Snork. "The Ant-lion is sure to come soon."

They waited again for an unbearably long time. The Snork Maiden hid her face in Moomintroll's lap, and Sniff whimpered with fright. Then suddenly, on the edge of the hat, appeared the world's smallest hedgehog. He sniffed the air and blinked, and he was very tangled and wet.

There was dead silence for a couple of seconds. Then Snufkin began to laugh, and in a very short time they were all howling and rolling about under the table in pure delight. All, that is, except the Hemulen

who did not join in the fun. He looked in surprise at his friends and said, "Well, we expected the Ant-lion to change, didn't we? If only I could understand why you always make such a fuss about things."

Meanwhile the little hedgehog had wandered solemnly and a little sadly to the door and out down the steps. The water had stopped flowing and now filled the verandah like a lake. And the whole ceiling was covered with Outlandish Words.

When the whole thing had been explained to Moominpappa and Moominmamma they took it very seriously, and decided that the Hobgoblin's Hat should be destroyed, so it was rolled cautiously down to the river and dropped into the water.

"There go the clouds and the magic changes," said Moominmamma as they watched the hat gliding away.

"The clouds were fun," said Moomintroll, rather dejectedly. "I shouldn't mind having *them* back!"

"And the flood and the Words, too, I suppose," Moominmamma said crossly. "Look at the verandah! And I can't think what I shall do with these little creeping Words. They're all over the place and making the whole house untidy."

"But the clouds *were* fun anyway," said Moomintroll obstinately. And that night he couldn't sleep, but lay looking out at the light June night which was full of lonely whisperings and rustlings and the pattering of feet. The air was sweet with the smell of flowers.

Snufkin wasn't in yet. On such nights he often wandered about alone with his mouth-organ, but tonight there was no song to be heard. He was probably on a voyage of discovery, and soon he would put up his tent by the river, refusing to sleep indoors. Moomintroll sighed. He felt sad but didn't know why.

Just then a faint whistle came from the garden. Moomintroll's heart gave a bound and he tiptoed softly to the window and looked out. The whistle meant: "Secrets!" Snufkin was waiting under the rope ladder.

"Can you keep a secret?" he whispered when Moomintroll had clambered down onto the grass.

Moomintroll nodded eagerly, and Snufkin leant towards him and whispered again: "The hat has floated to land on a sandbank down the river."

"What about it?" asked Snufkin's eyebrows, and Moomintroll's ears waggled a big "Yes." The next minute they were creeping like shadows through the dewy garden down toward the river.

"You know, it's really our duty to save the hat, because all the water that fills it is red," said Snufkin. "Those who live far down the river will be panic-stricken by all this awful water."

"We might have known something like that would happen," said Moomintroll. He felt very proud to be walking along like this with Snufkin in the middle of the night; Snufkin had always done his night wandering alone before.

"It's somewhere here," Snufkin said. "There's the dark streak in the water. Do you see?"

"Not properly," said Moomintroll, who was stumbling along in the half-dark. "I haven't got night-eyes like you."

"I wonder how we're going to get it," said Snufkin looking out over the river. "So foolish of your father not to have a boat."

Moomintroll hesitated. "I swim quite well—anyway if the water isn't too cold," he said.

"You wouldn't dare!" said Snufkin.

"I certainly would," Moomintroll retorted, suddenly feeling very brave. "Where is it now?"

"Across there," said Snufkin. "You'll soon touch bottom on the sandbank. But take care that you don't put your foot in the hat. Hold the crown of it."

Moomintroll slipped down into the warm summer

water and swam dog-wise out into the river. There was a strong current, and for a moment he felt a bit frightened. Then he saw the sandbank, with something black on it, and steering with his tail, he soon felt sand under his feet.

"Is everything all right?" called Snufkin from the shore, and an answering cry came from Moomintroll as he waded onto the sandbank.

There was a dark stream curling out of the hat and down to the river—it was the red water. Moomintroll stuck his paw into it and then licked it cautiously.

"Goodness gracious me," he muttered. "It's raspberry juice! Just think! From now on we can have as much raspberry juice as we want by just filling the hat with water." And his "Pee-Hoo!" war-cry went over the river to Snufkin, who shouted back impatiently, "Well, have you got it?"

"Oh, yes," Moomintroll shouted, wading into the water again with his tail in a firm knot round the Hobgoblin's Hat.

It is difficult to swim against the current with a heavy hat dragging behind you, and when Moomintroll struggled up the bank he was terribly tired.

"Here it is," he puffed proudly.

"Fine!" said Snufkin. "But now what shall we do with it?"

"Well, we can't keep it in Moominhouse," said Moomintroll. "Nor in the garden. Someone would find it."

At last they decided on the cave, but not to let Sniff into the secret (although it was really his cave), because he was rather a small person for such a big secret.

"You know," said Moomintroll seriously, "it's the

first time we have done anything that we couldn't tell Mother and Father about."

Snufkin took the hat in his arms and began going back by the river, but when they came to the bridge he suddenly stopped.

"What is it?" whispered Moomintroll in alarm.

"Canaries!" Snufkin burst out. "Three yellow canaries there on the bridge. How strange to see them out at night."

"I'm not a canary," peeped the nearest bird. "I'm a fish!"

"We are respectable fishes, all three!" his friend twittered.

Snufkin scratched his head.

"There—you see what the hat is getting up to," he said. "Those three little fishes were swimming in it, I'm sure, and were changed. Come on! We'll go straight to the cave and hide that hat!"

Moomintroll kept close behind Snufkin as they went through the wood. There were rustlings and patterings on both sides of the path and it was almost a bit frightening. Sometimes small, glittering eyes stared at them from behind the trees, and now and then something called to them from the ground or from the branches.

"A beautiful night!" Moomintroll heard a voice right behind him.

"Fine," he answered bravely. And a small shadow slunk past him in the dusk.

On the beach it was lighter. A pale blue shimmer

hung over the sea and sky, and far out the birds cried their lonely cries. Night was already over. Snufkin and Moomintroll carried the Hobgoblin's Hat up to the cave and put it, brim downward, in the darkest corner, so that nothing would be able to fall into it.

"Now we've done the best we can," said Snufkin. "And imagine if we could only get those five small clouds back!"

"Yes," said Moomintroll who stood in the opening of the cave looking out at the sea. "Though I wonder if they could make it any more wonderful than it is just now."

Chapter 3

*In which the Muskrat has a terrible experience;
how the Moomin family discover Hattifatteners'
Island where the Hemulen has a narrow escape,
and how they survive the great thunderstorm.*

Next morning the Muskrat went out as usual with
his book to lie in the hammock, but he had just
gotten comfortable when the string broke and he
found himself on the ground.

"Unpardonable!" exclaimed the Muskrat unwinding the rug from his legs.

"Oh, dear," said Moominpappa, who was watering
his tobacco plants. "I hope you didn't hurt yourself?"

"It isn't *that*," replied the Muskrat gloomily sucking
his moustache. "The earth can crack and fire come

down from heaven for all I care—that sort of thing doesn't disturb me—but I do not like to be put into a ridiculous situation. It isn't dignified for a philosopher!"

"But *I'm* the only one who saw it happen," protested Moominpappa.

"That's bad enough!" replied the Muskrat. "You will remember all that I have been exposed to in your house! Last year, for example, a comet fell on us. It was nothing. But as you perhaps remember, I sat on your wife's chocolate shape. It was the deepest insult to my dignity! And sometimes your guests put hair brushes in my bed—a particularly stupid joke. Not to mention your son, Moomintroll . . ."

"I know, I know," interrupted Moominpappa, miserably. "But there's no peace in this house . . . And sometimes string wears out with the years you know."

"It *must* not," said the Muskrat. "If I had killed myself, of course, it wouldn't have mattered. But imagine if your YOUNG PERSONS had seen me! Now, however, I intend to retire to a deserted spot and live a life of loneliness and peace, giving up everything. I have made up my mind once and for all."

Moominpappa was impressed. "Oh," he said. "Where will you go?"

"To the cave," said the Muskrat. "Nobody can interrupt my thoughts with stupid jokes there. You may bring me food twice a day. But not before ten o'clock."

"Good," said Moominpappa bowing. "And shall we bring you some furniture, too?"

"Yes, you can do that," said the Muskrat, more kindly. "But very simple things. I realize that you mean well, but that family of yours is really too much for me." So the Muskrat took his book and his rug and wandered slowly off toward the cliffs. Moominpappa sighed to himself; then he went on watering his tobacco plants and soon forgot all about it.

When the Muskrat arrived in the cave he was very pleased with everything. He spread out his rug on the sandy floor, sat down on it, and began at once to think. He continued to do that for about two hours. All was quiet and peaceful and through the crack in the roof the sun shone softly into his hiding place. Sometimes he moved slightly when the sun slid away from him.

"Here I shall stay forever and ever," he thought. "How unnecessary it is to run about and chatter, to build a house and cook food and collect possessions!" He looked contentedly around his new home, and then he caught sight of the Hobgoblin's Hat, which Moomintroll and Snufkin had hidden in the darkest corner.

"The wastepaper basket," said the Muskrat to himself. "Oh, so it's here. Well, it will always come in useful."

He thought a little while longer, and then he decided to sleep for a bit. He rolled himself in the blanket and put his false teeth in the hat so that they

would not get sandy. Then he slept peacefully and happily.

In Moominhouse they had pancakes for lunch—big yellow pancakes with raspberry jam. There was porridge from the day before as well, but as nobody wanted it they decided to save it for the next morning.

"Today I feel like doing something unusual," said Moominmamma. "The fact that we have got rid of that awful hat is something that ought to be celebrated, and besides one gets so tired of everlast-ingly sitting in the same place."

"That's quite true, my dear!" said Moominpappa. "We'll go on an excursion somewhere, what!"

"We've been everywhere already. There isn't anywhere new," said the Hemulen.

"But there must be," said Moominpappa. "And if there isn't, then we'll make somewhere. Stop eating now, children—we'll take the food with us."

"Can we eat what we already have in our mouths?" asked Sniff.

"Don't be silly, dear," said Moominmamma. "Col-lect everything you want to take with you quickly, because Father wants to start at once. But don't take anything unnecessary. We can write a note to the Muskrat so that he knows where we are."

"Bless my tail!" burst out Moominpappa, and put his hand to his forehead. "I had completely forgotten! We should have taken food and furniture to him in the cave!"

"In the *cave*?" screamed Moomintroll and Snufkin at the same time.

"Yes—the string of the hammock gave out," said Moominpappa. "And so the Muskrat said that he couldn't think anymore, and that he would give up everything. You had put brushes in his bed, and I don't know what. And so he went away to the cave."

Moomintroll and Snufkin went very pale and looked at each other in horror. "The Hat!" they thought.

"Well, it doesn't matter very much," said Moomin-mamma. "We'll go on an excursion to the beach and take the Muskrat's food to him on the way."

"The beach is so ordinary," grumbled Sniff. "Can't we go somewhere else?"

"Be quiet, children!" said Moominpappa, severely. "Mamma wants to swim. Now, come along!"

Moominmamma hurried off to pack. She collected blankets, saucepans, birch bark,* a coffeepot, masses of food, suntan oil, matches, and everything you can eat out of, on or with. She packed it all with an umbrella, warm clothes, tummy-ache medicine, an egg-whisk, cushions, a mosquito net, bathing-trunks and a tablecloth in her bag. She bustled to and fro racking her brains for anything she had forgotten,

---

*Birch bark is the best thing for starting a fire, and you must be prepared for any emergency on an excursion. *Author.*

and at last she said, "Now it's ready! Oh, how lovely it will be to have a rest by the sea!"

Moominpappa packed his pipe and his fishing-rod.

"Well, are you all ready?" he asked. "And are you sure you haven't forgotten anything? All right, let's start!"

They set off in a procession toward the beach. Last of all came Sniff dragging six little toy boats behind him.

"Do you think the Muskrat has got up to anything?" whispered Moomintroll to Snufkin.

"I certainly hope not!" Snufkin whispered back. "But I'm feeling a bit anxious!"

At that moment they all stopped so suddenly that the Hemulen nearly got the fishing-rod in his eye.

"Who screamed?" Moominmamma burst out in alarm.

The whole wood shook with a wild howling, and someone or something came galloping towards them on the path, growling with terror and rage.

"Hide!" shouted Moominpappa. "There's a monster coming!"

But before anyone had time to move the monster turned out to be the Muskrat, with staring eyes and bristling whiskers. He waved his paws and made incoherent sounds that nobody could understand, but it was clear that he was very angry or frightened, or angry because he was frightened. Then he turned tail and fled.

"What *has* happened to the Muskrat?" said Moomin-mamma, anxiously. "He was always so calm and dignified!"

"To get into such a state just because the hammock cord broke!" said Moominpappa shaking his head.

"I think he was angry because we forgot to take food to him," said Sniff. "Now we can eat it ourselves."

They continued their way to the beach a bit disturbed in their thoughts. But Moomintroll and Snufkin sneaked off in front of the others and took a short cut to the cave.

"We daren't go in through the door—perhaps the Thing is still there!" said Snufkin. "We'll climb up on top and look down through the crack in the roof."

Quietly they crawled up, worming their way like Indians toward the opening in the roof, and looked down into the cave. There stood the Hobgoblin's Hat, and it was empty. The rug was thrown in one corner—the book in another. The cave was deserted. But everywhere in the sand strange footprints could be seen, as if someone had been dancing and jumping about.

"It wasn't the Muskrat's paws that made those footprints," said Moomintroll.

"I wonder if it was some other paws," said Snufkin. "It looks awfully queer." They clambered down again and looked nervously around.

But nothing alarming happened.

They never found out what had frightened the

Muskrat so terribly, because he refused to talk about it.*

But meanwhile the others had arrived on the beach. They all stood in a bunch down by the water's edge chattering and waving their arms.

"They've found a boat!" cried Snufkin. "Come on! Let's run and see!"

It was true. A lovely big sailing boat, complete with oars and fishing tackle, and painted in white and mauve!

"Whose is it?" panted Moomintroll when he had reached them.

"Nobody's!" said Moominpappa, triumphantly. "It has been washed up on our beach, so we have a right to keep it as wreckage!"

"It must have a name!" cried the Snork Maiden. "Wouldn't *The Pee-wit* be rather sweet?"

"Pee-wit yourself," said the Snork rudely. "I prefer *The Sea Eagle*."

"No, it must be Latin," cried the Hemulen. "*Moomin-ates Maritima*."

"I saw it first!" squeaked Sniff. "*I* must choose a name for it. Wouldn't it be fun to call it *SNIFF*? That's so short and sweet."

"Just like you—I *don't* think!" said Moomintroll, jeeringly.

"Hush, children!" said Moominpappa. "Quiet,

---

*If you want to find out what the Muskrat's false teeth were changed into you can ask your Mamma. She is sure to know. *Author*.

quiet! Obviously Mamma will choose the name. It's her excursion."

Moominmamma blushed a little. "If only I could!" she said, shyly. "Snufkin has such an imagination. I'm sure he will choose much better."

Snufkin was rather flattered. "Well! I don't know," he said. "But to tell you the truth, I thought from the beginning that *Lurking Wolf* would be rather nice."

"Get away with you," said Moomintroll. "Mother shall choose."

"Yes dears," said Moominmamma. "Only you mustn't think I'm stupid and old-fashioned. I think the boat should be called something to remind us all of what we are going to do with her—and so I think *The Adventure* would be a good name."

"Marvelous!" shouted Moomintroll. "We'll christen her! Have you anything we can use for a bottle of champagne, mother?"

Moominmamma hunted in all her baskets for a bottle of raspberry juice.

"Oh dear, how sad!" she burst out. "I think I've forgotten the raspberry juice!"

"Well, I asked you if you had everything, didn't I, my dear?" said Moominpappa, virtuously.

They all looked at each other sadly. To sail away in a boat that hasn't been properly christened can mean the worst possible luck.

Then Moomintroll had a brilliant idea. "Give me a saucepan," he said. Then he filled it with sea water and carried it up to the cave and the Hobgoblin's

Hat. When he came back he handed some raspberry juice to his father and said: "Taste this!"

Moominpappa took a gulp and looked very pleased. "Where did you get this from, my boy?" he asked.

But Moomintroll said it was a secret, so they filled a bottle with the juice and broke it against the prow of the sailing boat, while Moominmamma proudly proclaimed, "Herewith I christen you now and forever *The Adventure*."

Everybody cheered, and then they put the baskets, blankets, umbrella, fishing rod, cushions, saucepans and bathing suits on board, and the Moomin family and their friends set sail for the wild, green sea.

It was a fine day. Perhaps not quite clear, because a gold haze lay over the sun, but *The Adventure* spread her white sails and headed out to sea at a good speed. The waves slapped the sides of the boat and the wind sang, and mermaids and mermen danced around the bows, while big white birds circled up above.

Sniff had tied his six little boats in a line, one after the other, and now the whole fleet sailed in *The Adventure*'s wake. Moominpappa steered and Moominmamma sat dozing. It was seldom she had such peace around her.

"Where shall we go?" asked the Snork.

"Let's go to an island!" begged the Snork Maiden. "I've never been to a little island before."

"You shall do it now," said Moominpappa. "We'll land on the first island we see."

Moomintroll was sitting farthest up in the bows keeping a lookout for reefs. It was so wonderful to stare down into the green depths and watch *The Adventure*'s prow cutting through the white foam.

"Pee-Hoo!" shouted Moomintroll. "We're going to an island!"

Far out to sea lay the Hattifatteners' Lonely Island, surrounded by reefs and breakers. (Once a year the Hattifatteners collect there before setting out again on their endless foraging expedition round the world. They come from all points of the compass, silent and serious with their small, white empty faces, and why they hold this yearly meeting it is difficult to say, as they can neither hear nor speak, and have no object in life but the distant goal of their journey's end. Perhaps they like to have a place where they feel at home and can rest a little and meet friends. The yearly meeting is always in June, and thus it was that the Moomin family and the Hattifatteners arrived on Lonely Island at about the same time.) Wild and tempting it rose from the sea, wreathed in white breakers and crowned with green trees as if dressed for a gala.

"Land ahead!" shouted Moomintroll, and they all hung over the rail to look.

"There's a sandy beach," cried the Snork Maiden.

"And a fine harbor!" cried Moominpappa, steering skilfully in to land between the reefs. *The Adventure* ran deep into the sand, and Moomintroll jumped ashore with the painter.

The beach was soon seething with activity. Moomin-mamma dragged up some stones to make a fireplace to warm up the pancakes; she collected wood and spread out the tablecloth with a little stone on each corner to stop it blowing away; she put out all the cups and sunk the butter jar in the wet sand in the shade of a stone, and finally she arranged a bouquet of beach-lilies in the middle of the table.

"Can we help you with anything?" asked Moomin-troll, when everything was ready.

"You can explore the island," said Moominmamma (who knew that was what they were longing to do). "It's important to know where we've landed. It could be dangerous, couldn't it?"

"Exactly," said Moomintroll. And off he went with the Snork Maiden and her brother and Sniff toward the south shore, while Snufkin, who loved to dis-cover things alone, set off for the north. The Hemu-len took his botanizing-spade, his green collecting tin and his magnifying glass, and wandered into the wood. He thought he might find some wonderful vegetation that nobody had yet discovered.

Meanwhile Moominpappa sat down on a stone to fish. And the sun sank slowly down while the golden haze blotted out the sea.

In the middle of the island lay a green glade with a smooth floor, surrounded by flowering shrubs. Here the Hattifatteners had their secret meeting place where they gathered once a year at mid-summer. About three hundred of them had already found

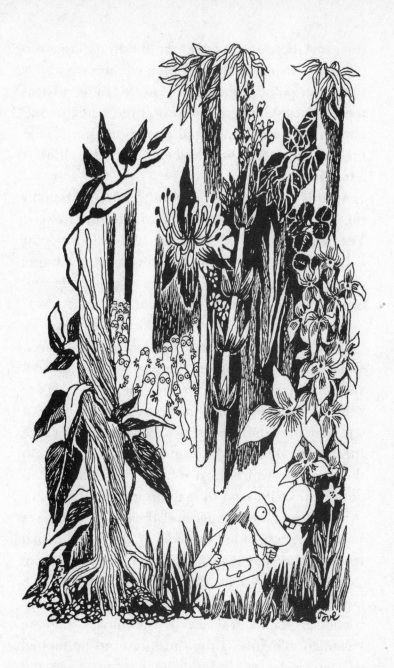

their way there and at least four hundred more were expected. In the middle of the glade they had put up a high pole, painted blue. On this hung a barometer. They skimmed silently over the grass bowing haughtily to each other, and every time they passed the barometer they bowed deeply to it. (This looked a bit ridiculous.)

All this time the Hemulen was rambling about in the wood, enraptured by the masses of rare flowers. They were not like the flowers that grew in Moomin Valley—oh, far from it! Heavy, silvery-white clusters which looked as if they were made of glass; crimson-black kingcups like royal crowns, and sky-blue roses.

But the Hemulen didn't see much of their beauty—he was too busy counting the stamens and leaves, and muttering to himself, "This is the two hundred-and-nineteenth specimen in my collection!"

Eventually he reached the Hattifatteners' hideout and wandered into it peering eagerly around for rare specimens. He didn't look up until he bumped into the blue pole, which startled him very much. He had never in his life seen so many Hattifatteners! They swarmed over everything and their pale little eyes stared through him. "I wonder if they're in a bad temper," the Hemulen thought to himself. "They're small, but there are horribly many of them!"

He looked at the big, shiny mahogany barometer. It stood at "Rain and Wind." "Extraordinary," said the Hemulen, blinking at the sunshine, and he tapped the barometer which sunk quite a bit. Then the

Hattifatteners rustled threateningly and took a step toward him.

"It's all right," he said in alarm. "I won't take your barometer!"

But the Hattifatteners didn't hear him. They just came nearer, rustling and waving their hands. The Hemulen, with his heart in his mouth, watched for an opportunity to make his escape, but the enemy stood like a wall around him and always came nearer. And between the trees came still more Hattifatteners, with their staring eyes and silent tread. "Go away!" screamed the Hemulen. "Shoo! Shoo!"

But still they came silently nearer. Then the Hemulen picked up his skirts and began to climb up the pole. It was nasty and slippery, but terror gave him un-Hemulenish strength, and at last he reached the top and got hold of the barometer.

The Hattifatteners had now reached the foot of the pole and there they waited. The whole glade was thick with them, like a white carpet, and the Hemulen felt quite ill when he thought of what would happen if he fell down.

"Help!" he yelled at the top of his voice. "Help! Help!" But the wood was silent.

Then he stuck two fingers in his mouth and whistled. Three short, three long, three short. S.O.S.

Snufkin, who had wandered along the beach, heard the Hemulen's signal of distress and lifted his head to listen. When he had got the direction clear he dashed to the rescue. The call became louder, and Snufkin, realizing that now it was quite near, crept cautiously forward. It became lighter between the trees, and then he saw the glade, the Hattifatteners, and the Hemulen clutching on tightly to the pole. "This is a terrible situation," he muttered to himself, and then louder to the Hemulen, "Hi! However did you get the peaceful Hattifatteners into such a warlike frame of mind?"

"I only tapped their barometer," moaned the poor Hemulen. "And it sunk. Try to take the nasty creatures away, dear Snufkin!"

"I must think a bit," said Snufkin.

(The Hattifatteners heard nothing of these remarks because they hadn't any ears).

After a time the Hemulen shouted, "Think quickly, Snufkin, because I'm beginning to slip down!"

"Listen!" said Snufkin. "Do you remember the time when those voles came into the garden? Moominpappa dug a lot of poles into the ground and put windmills on them. And when the wheels went around the earth shook so much that the voles were nervous and gave up!"

"Your stories are always very interesting," said the Hemulen, bitterly. "But I can't understand what they have to do with my sad predicament!"

"A good deal!" said Snufkin. "Don't you see? The Hattifatteners can neither talk nor hear, and they see very badly. But they can feel extremely well! Try to

jerk the pole backward and forward. The Hattifatteners will feel it in the ground and be frightened. It
goes right up into their tummies, you see! They're
like radio sets!"

The Hemulen tried to swing to and fro on the
pole.

"I'm falling down!" he burst out in alarm.

"Faster, faster!" cried Snufkin. "Tiny little move-
ments."

The Hemulen managed a few more desperate
rocks, and then the Hattifatteners began to feel uncomfortable in the soles of their feet. They began to
rustle and to move anxiously about. And the next
minute, just as the voles had done, they took to their
heels and ran.

In a couple of seconds the glade was empty.
Snufkin felt them against his legs as they scattered
into the wood, and they stung him rather like nettles.

The Hemulen slid down onto the grass completely
exhausted.

"Oh!" he moaned. "There has never been anything but trouble and danger since I came into the
Moomin family."

"Do calm yourself, Hemul," said Snufkin. "After
all you've been pretty lucky."

"Wretched Hatti-creatures," grumbled the Hemulen. "I shall take their barometer with me anyhow, to
punish them."

"Better let it be," warned Snufkin.

But the Hemulen unhooked the big, shiny barometer from the pole and stuck it triumphantly under his arm.

"Now we'll go back to the others," he said. "I'm awfully hungry."

When they arrived all the others were eating pancakes, and tuna fish which Moominpappa had caught in the sea.

"Hi!" cried Moomintroll. "We've been around the whole island, and on the farther side there is a dreadful wild cliff that goes right down into the sea."

"And we've seen a mass of Hattifatteners!" Sniff told them. "At least a hundred!"

"Don't mention those creatures again," said the Hemulen with deep feeling. "I can't stand it. But here, come and see my war trophy." And he proudly put the barometer in the middle of the tablecloth.

"Oh! So bright and beautiful!" exclaimed the Snork Maiden. "Is it a clock?"

"No, it's a barometer," said Moominpappa. "It tells you what the weather will be. A low reading means 'stormy.' Sometimes it's quite right." And he tapped the barometer. Then he put his face into a serious crease and said, "It *is* stormy!"

"A big storm?" asked Sniff anxiously.

"Look for yourself," replied Moominpappa. "The barometer points to the lowest a barometer can point to—if it isn't fooling us."

But it certainly didn't look as if it were fooling. The

golden mist had thickened to a yellow-grey fog, and out toward the horizon the sea was strangely black.

"We must go home!" said the Snork.

"Not yet!" begged the Snork Maiden. "We haven't had time to explore the cliff on the other side properly! We haven't even gone swimming!"

"We can wait a little and see what happens, can't we?" said Moomintroll. "It would be such a pity to go home just when we've discovered this island!"

"But if there's a storm we shan't be able to go at all!" said the Snork, brightly.

"That would be wonderful!" burst out Sniff. "We could stay here for ever and ever."

"Quiet, children, I must think," said Moominpappa. He went down to the beach and sniffed the air, turned his head in all directions and wrinkled his forehead.

There was a rumble in the distance.

"Thunder!" said Sniff. "Ooh, how awful!"

Over the horizon loomed a threatening bank of cloud. It was dark blue and drove little light puffy clouds in front of it. Now and then a great flash of lightning lit up the sea.

"We stay," decided Moominpappa.

"The whole night?" squeaked Sniff.

"I think so," Moominpappa replied. "Hurry up now and build a house, as the rain will come soon."

The Adventure was dragged high up onto the sand, and on the edge of the wood they quickly made a house with the sail and some blankets. Moomin-mamma filled up the gaps with moss, and the Snork dug a ditch round it so that the rainwater would have somewhere to go. Everybody ran to and fro putting their things safely under cover, while the thunder rolled nearer and a little wind came sighing anxiously through the trees.

"I'll go and see what the weather's like out on the point," said Snufkin, and, pulling his hat firmly down over his ears, he set off. Alone and happy he ran out to the farthermost point of rock and put his back against a large boulder.

The sea had changed. It was dark green now with white-horses, and the rocks shone yellow like phosphorus. Rumbling solemnly, the thunderstorm came up from the south. It spread its black sail over the sea; it spread over half the sky and the lightning flashed with an ominous glint.

"It's coming right over the island," thought Snufkin with a thrill of joy and excitement. He imagined he was sailing high up over the clouds, and perhaps shooting out to sea on a hissing flash of lightning.

Now the sun had gone, and the rain was driving like a grey curtain over the sea. Though it was still many hours till evening the whole world was shrouded in darkness.

Snufkin turned, and skipped back over the stones. He just reached the tent in time, for heavy drops of rain were already hitting the sailcloth and it was being whipped about in the wind. Sniff had rolled

himself completely in a blanket as he was rather afraid of thunder, and the others sat hunched-up next to one another. The tent smelt strongly of the Hemulen's botanical specimens.

Now there was a terrific clap of thunder right over their heads and their little refuge was lit again and again by flashes of white light. The thunder rumbled round the sky like a great train while the sea hurled its biggest waves against Lonely Island.

"What a blessing we aren't on the sea," said Moominmamma. "Dear me, what weather!"

The Snork Maiden put her trembling paw in Moomintroll's, and he felt very protecting and manly.

Sniff lay under his blanket and screamed.

"Now it's right over us!" said Moominpappa. And at that moment a giant flash of lightning lit up the island, followed by a rending crash.

"That struck something!" said the Snork.

It was really a bit too much. The Hemulen sat holding his head. "Trouble! Always trouble!" he muttered.

Now it began to move off to the south. The thunder claps got farther and farther away, the lightning became fainter, and at last there was only the rustle of the rain and the sound of the sea as it broke on the shore.

"You can come out now, Sniff," said Snufkin. "It's all over."

Sniff disentangled himself from the blanket, yawned and scratched his ear. He was a bit embarrassed because he had made such a fuss. "What's the time?" he asked.

"Nearly eight," answered the Snork.

"Then I think we'll go and lie down," said Moominmamma. "All this has been very disturbing."

"But wouldn't it be exciting to find out what the lightning struck?" said Moomintroll.

"In the morning!" said his mother. "In the

morning we'll explore everything and have a swim. Now the island is wet and grey and unpleasant." She tucked them up and then went to sleep herself with her handbag under her pillow.

Outside the storm redoubled its fury. The voice of the waves was now mixed with strange sounds; laughter, running feet and the clanging of great bells far out to sea. Snufkin lay still and listened, dreaming and remembering his trip around the world. "Soon I must set out again," he thought. "But not yet."

Chapter 4

*In which owing to the Hattifatteners' night
attack the Snork Maiden loses her hair,
and in which the most remarkable discovery
is made on Lonely Island.*

In the middle of the night the Snork Maiden woke up with an awful feeling. Something had touched her face. She didn't dare to look but sniffed uneasily around her. There was a smell of burning, so she pulled the blanket over her head and called tremulously to Moomintroll.

He woke up at once and asked her what was the matter.

"There's something dangerous in here," came a muffled voice from under the blanket. "I can *feel* it."

Moomintroll stared into the darkness. There *was* something! Little lights . . . Pale gleaming shapes that pattered to and fro between the sleepers. Moomintroll was terrified and woke Snufkin.

"Look!" he gasped. "Ghosts!"

"It's all right," said Snufkin. "Those are Hattifatteners. The thundery weather has electrified them—that's why they shine so. Keep quite still, otherwise you might get an electric shock."

The Hattifatteners seemed to be looking for something. They poked about in all the hampers, and the burning smell became stronger, and then suddenly they all collected in the corner where the Hemulen was sleeping.

"Do you think they're after him?" asked Moomintroll, anxiously.

"They're probably only looking for the barometer," said Snufkin. "I warned him not to take it. Now they've found it."

The Hattifatteners were all clinging to the barometer and had clambered up onto the Hemulen so as to reach it better; the smell of burning was very strong now.

Sniff woke up and began to whimper, and at the same time there was a piercing scream. A Hattifattener had trodden on the Hemulen's nose.

In a moment everybody was awake and on their feet. Pandemonium broke loose. Hattifatteners were trodden on; Sniff got an electric shock; the Hemulen rushed about screaming with terror, and then entangled himself in the sail so that the whole tent collapsed on top of them. It was quite frightful.

Sniff maintained afterward that it was at least an hour before they had found their way out of the sail. (Perhaps he exaggerated a bit.)

But by the time they had all sorted themselves out the Hattifatteners had disappeared into the wood with the barometer. And nobody had the least desire to follow them.

The Hemulen, moaning piteously, thrust his nose into the sand. "This has gone too far!" he said. "Why can't a poor innocent botanist live his life in peace and quiet?"

"Life is not peaceful," said Snufkin, contentedly.

"Look, children!" said Moominpappa, "it has cleared up. Soon it'll begin to get light."

Moominmamma shivered and clutched her handbag tight as she looked out over the stormy night sea. "Shall we build a new house and try to sleep again?" she asked.

"That wouldn't be any use," said Moomintroll. "We'll wrap ourselves up in the blankets and wait till the sun gets up."

So they sat in a row on the beach, very close to one another, and Sniff sat in the middle because he thought it was safest.

The night was nearly over now and the storm was far away, but the breakers still thundered in over the sand. The sky began to grow pale in the east and it was very cold. Then, in the first light of dawn, they

saw the Hattifatteners setting off from the island.
Boatloads of them glided away like shadows from
behind the point and steered out to sea.

The Hemulen breathed a sigh of relief. "I hope I
never see a Hattifattener again," he said.

"They're probably looking for a new island for themselves," said Snufkin, enviously. "A secret island that
nobody will ever find!" And he followed the little
boats with longing eyes.

The Snork Maiden was sleeping with her head in
Moomintroll's lap when the first golden streak
showed on the eastern horizon. A few little puffs of
cloud that the storm had forgotten turned a soft
shell pink, and then the sun lifted his shining head
over the sea.

Moomintroll bent down to wake the Snork Maiden

up, and then he noticed a terrible thing. Her beautiful fluffy fringe was burnt right off. It must have happened when the Hattifatteners brushed against her. What would she say? How could he comfort her? It was a catastrophe!

The Snork Maiden opened her eyes and smiled.

"Do you know," said Moomintroll hastily, "it's most extraordinary, but as time goes on I'm beginning to prefer girls without hair?"

"Really?" she said with a look of surprise. "Why is that?"

"Hair looks so untidy!" replied Moomintroll.

The Snork Maiden immediately lifted her paw to pat her hair—but alas! All she got hold of was a little burnt tuft, which she stared at in horror.

"You've gone bald," said Sniff.

"It suits you—really," Moomintroll said, consolingly. "Please don't cry!"

But the Snork Maiden threw herself down on the sand and wept bitterly over the loss of her crowning glory.

They all crowded round trying to cheer her up—but in vain.

"Listen," said the Hemulen. "I was born bald on top and really I get along very well."

"We'll rub your head with oil so that it's sure to grow again," said Moominpappa.

"And then it will be so curly!" added Moominmamma.

"Will it really?" sobbed the Snork Maiden.

"Of *course* it will," soothed Moominmamma. "Think how sweet you'll look with curly hair!" So the Snork Maiden stopped crying and sat up.

"Look how lovely it is!" said Snufkin. The island had been washed by the rain and now sparkled in the early morning sunlight. "I shall play a morning song," he went on taking out his mouth-organ. So they all sang lustily after him:

> There's no need to worry or fear or fret:
> There's plenty of life in all of us yet.
> The Hattifatteners, every one,
> Have sailed away to the rising sun.
> And after beauty we'll never more crave,
> For the Snork Maiden's getting a permanent
>   wave.

"Come and swim!" cried Moomintroll. And the whole lot pulled on their swimming suits and rushed out into the breakers (except the Hemulen and Moominmamma and Pappa who thought it was still too cold).

Glass-green and white waves rolled in over the sand. Oh, to be a Moomin and to dance in the waves while the sun gets up! The night was forgotten and a long June day lay before them. They dived like porpoises through the waves and sailed in on the crests towards the beach where Sniff was playing in the shallow water. Snufkin was floating on his back far out and looking up into the blue and gold sky.

Meanwhile Moominmamma was making coffee and looking for the butter jar which she had hidden from the sun in the damp sand. But she looked in vain—the storm had washed it away. "Oh dear, what can I give them for sandwiches?" she wailed.

"Never mind," said Moominpappa. "We'll see if the storm has given us something else instead. After coffee we'll make a tour of inspection along the beach and see what the sea has washed up!" And this they did.

On the farther side of the island shining slippery rocks reared up out of the sea and there you could find both patches of shell-strewn sand (the mermaids' private dance floors) and secret black chasms into which the breakers thundered, as though they were battering on an iron door; in fact there were caves and gurgling whirlpools and all manner of exciting things to be found.

Everyone set out on his own to see what had been washed up. (This is the most exciting occupation, for you can find the strangest things, and it is often quite difficult and dangerous to save them from the sea.)

Moominmamma clambered down to a little patch of sand which was hidden by some fearsome rocks. Here clumps of blue sea-pinks grew and the sea-oats rattled and whistled as the wind forced its way up their narrow stalks. She lay down in a sheltered spot from which she could see only the blue sky and the sea-pinks that waved over her head. "I'll rest just a little while," she thought, but soon she was fast asleep in the warm sand.

But the Snork ran to the top of the highest hill and looked around. He could see from shore to shore, and the island seemed to him to float like a giant water lily on the uneasy sea. He saw Sniff—just a speck—looking for wreckage; he even caught sight of Snufkin's hat; and surely that was the Hemulen digging up a rare shell-orchid . . . And there! Wasn't that where the lightning had struck? A terrible crag, bigger than ten Moominhouses, had been split like an apple by the lightning, and the two halves had fallen apart leaving a deep cleft between them. The Snork climbed trembling into the crack and looked up at the dark cliff walls which the lightning had split open. The stone was as black as ebony, but through it ran a bright and shining streak. It was gold—it must be gold!

The Snork poked about with his penknife. A little grain of gold came loose and fell into his paw. He picked out one piece after another, getting hot with excitement and digging out bigger and bigger pieces. After a time he had forgotten everything but the brilliant vein of gold which the lightning had brought to light. He wasn't a beachcomber any longer—he was a gold-digger!

Meanwhile Sniff had made a very simple find, but he was just as happy over it. He had found a life belt. It was slightly rotted by sea water, but it fitted him perfectly. "Now I can go into the deep water," he thought, "and I'm sure I shall soon be able to swim as well as the others. Won't Moomintroll be surprised!" A little farther away, amongst the birch bark, floats, and seaweed, he discovered a raffia mat, a broken dipper, and an old boot without a heel. Wonderful treasures when you steal them from the sea! Then in the distance he caught sight of Moomintroll, who was standing out in the water struggling with something. Something big! "What a pity that I didn't see it first!" thought Sniff. "What in the world can it be?"

Now Moomintroll had got his find out of the water and was rolling it in front of him up the beach. Sniff craned his neck—and then he saw what it was. A buoy! A big and gorgeous buoy!

"Pee-hoo!" shouted Moomintroll. "What do you think of this?"

"It's quite nice," said Sniff, critically, with his head on one side. "But what do you think of this?" And he displayed *his* find on the sand.

"The life belt is lovely," replied Moomintroll. "But what's the use of half a dipper?"

"It will probably do if you bail quickly," said Sniff. "Listen! What do you say to a swap? The raffia mat, the dipper, and the boot for that old buoy?"

"Never in your life!" said Moomintroll. "But perhaps the life belt for this rarey object that must have drifted here from a distant land." And he held up a glass ball and shook it. Then up whirled a mass of snowflakes inside settling gradually to rest on a little house with windows of silver paper.

"Oh!" said Sniff. And a great struggle was going on inside him because he couldn't bear to part with anything, even in exchange.

"Look!" said Moomintroll and shook the snow up again.

"I don't know," said Sniff, doubtfully. "I don't really know which I like best, the life belt or your snowstorm."

"I'm pretty sure it's the only one in the world at the moment," said Moomintroll.

"But I *can't* give up the life belt!" wailed Sniff. "Dear Moomintroll, couldn't we share the little snowstorm?"

"Hm," said Moomintroll.

"Couldn't I just hold it sometimes?" begged Sniff. "On Sundays?"

Moomintroll thought for a bit, and then he said, "Well, all right! You can have it on Sundays and Wednesdays."

Meanwhile Snufkin was wandering along with only the waves for company. He had a wonderful time jumping out of their way at the last minute, and laughing as they snapped in vain at his boots.

Just beyond the point he met Moominpappa, who was salvaging driftwood.

"Fine, eh?" he puffed. "We can build a landing-stage for *The Adventure* with this!"

"Shall I help you to drag it up?" asked Snufkin.

"No, no!" said Moominpappa, a little shocked. "I can manage it alone. Can't you find something of your own to drag up?"

There was a great deal to be salvaged, but nothing

that Snufkin cared about. Small barrels, half a chair, a basket without a bottom, an ironing board; heavy troublesome things. Snufkin stuck his hands in his pockets and whistled. He preferred teasing the waves.

But out on the point the Snork Maiden was clambering about on the rocks. She had decorated her singed brow with a crown of sea lilies, and was searching for something that would surprise all the others and make them jealous. When they had admired it she would give it to Moomintroll, as long as it wasn't something she could use to make herself beautiful. It was bothersome climbing about on the stones, and her crown was beginning to blow off. But at any rate the wind wasn't so strong now, and the sea had changed from an angry green to a peaceful blue; the waves no longer seemed threatening, but tossed their plumes with a gay air. The Snork Maiden climbed down onto a little pebbly beach which bordered the water's edge, but there was nothing to be seen except a little seaweed and some bits of driftwood. A little downhearted she strolled farther out on the point. "It's sad that everyone except me does so much," thought the Snork Maiden to herself. "They retrieve magic hats, capture ant-lions and carry off barometers. I wish I could do something tremendous, all on my own, and impress Moomintroll."

Sighing to herself she looked out over the deserted beach. And then her heart nearly stopped beating for out on the point a Shape was washing to

and fro in the shallow water! And it was tremen-
dously big—ten times as big as a little Snork
Maiden!

"I'll run and fetch the others at once," she thought,
and then stopped, telling herself not to be frightened but to have a look and see what it was. So, trembling in every limb, she went up to the awful thing to
find it was nothing less than a giantess—a giantess
without legs! How terrible! The Snork Maiden took
a few shaky steps forward, but then came the biggest
surprise of all—the giantess was made of wood, and
she was very beautiful. Her cheeks and lips were
red and her round blue eyes smiled up through the

clear water; she had blue hair, too, flowing in long painted curls over her shoulders. "It's a queen," said the Snork Maiden, reverently. The beautiful creature's hands were crossed on her breast which was hung with golden flowers and chains. Her dress was of soft flowing red material, and she was all of painted wood. The only strange thing was that she hadn't got a back.

"She is almost too good for Moomintroll," mused the Snork Maiden. "But he shall have her in any case!" And she was very proud when, toward evening, she paddled into the harbor perched on the queen's middle.

"Have you found a *boat*?" asked the Snork.

"Fancy your being able to find it all alone," said Moomintroll, admiringly.

"It's a figurehead," said Moominpappa, who in his youth had sailed the seven seas. "Sailors like to decorate the prows of their ships with a beautiful wooden queen."

"What for?" asked Sniff.

"Oh, I suppose they like ladies," said Moominpappa.

"But why hasn't she got a back?" asked the Hemulen.

"That's where she's fixed to the ship's prow of course," said the Snork. "Even a child could see that!"

"She's too big to be nailed to *The Adventure*," said Snufkin. "What a pity!"

"Oh, what a beautiful lady!" sighed Moomin-mamma. "Imagine being so pretty and getting no happiness out of it!"

"What do you think of doing with it?" asked Sniff.

The Snork Maiden lowered her eyes and smiled. Then she said, "I think I shall give it to Moomin-troll."

Moomintroll was speechless. Very pink in the face, he advanced and bowed. The Snork Maiden curt-sied shyly, and they were both rather embarrassed.

"Look!" said the Snork to his sister. "You haven't seen what *I've* found!" And he pointed proudly to a great pile of shimmering gold that lay on the sand.

The Snork Maiden's eyes nearly popped out. "Real gold!" she breathed.

"And there's lots more," boasted the Snork. "A mountain of gold!"

"And *I'm* allowed to keep all the bits he drops!" said Sniff, proudly.

Oh, how they admired each other's finds there on the beach! The Moomin family had suddenly be-come rich. But the most precious things were still the ship's figurehead and the little snowstorm in the glass ball. The boat was indeed heavily laden when she sailed away from Lonely Island after the storm. Behind her floated a big raft carrying the driftwood they had collected. Their cargo consisted of the gold and the little snowstorm, of the gorgeous big buoy, the boot, the dipper, the life belt, and the raffia mat,

and in the prow lay the figurehead gazing out to sea. Beside her sat Moomintroll with his paw on her beautiful blue hair. He was so happy!

The Snork Maiden couldn't keep her eyes off them.

"Oh, if only I were as beautiful as the Wooden Queen," she thought, "but I haven't even got my fringe left." And she didn't feel gay anymore.

"Do you like the Wooden Queen?" she asked Moomintroll.

"*Very* much!" he answered without looking up.

"But I thought you said you didn't approve of girls with hair," said the Snork Maiden. "Besides she's only painted!"

"But so beautifully painted!" said Moomintroll.

This was almost too much for the Snork Maiden. She stared down into the sea with a lump in her throat and went very pale. "The Wooden Queen looks so stupid!" she said at last.

Then Moomintroll looked up.

"Why are you so pale?" he asked in surprise.

"Oh, nothing in particular!" she answered.

Then he clambered down from the prow and sat beside her, and after a while he said, "Do you know, the Wooden Queen looks terribly stupid actually."

"She *does*, doesn't she?" said the Snork Maiden, getting her color back again.

"Do you remember the golden butterfly we saw?" asked Moomintroll, and the Snork Maiden nodded, tired and happy.

Far away Lonely Island lay flaming in the light of the sunset.

"I wonder what you're all thinking of doing with the Snork's gold?" said Snufkin.

"I think we shall use it to decorate the edges of the flower beds," said Moominmamma, "only the big bits, of course, because the little ones look so rubbishy."

Then in silence they watched the sun dive into the sea, and the colors fade to blue and violet, while *The Adventure* rocked gently homeward.

Chapter 5

*In which we hear of the Mameluke Hunt, and
of how the Moominhouse is changed
into a jungle.*

I t was somewhere about the end of July and very
hot in Moomin Valley. Not even the flies bothered to buzz. The trees seemed to be tired; the
river was no longer fit for raspberry juice but flowed
narrow and brown through the dusty countryside.
The Hobgoblin's Hat, which had been taken back
into favor, stood on the chest of drawers under the
mirror.

Day after day the sun beat down on the little valley lying hidden between the hills. The small creeping things hid themselves in the cool darkness; the

birds were silent, and Moomintroll and his friends got peevish and quarreled amongst themselves.

"Mother," said Moomintroll. "Find us something to do! We just quarrel, and it's so hot!"

"Yes, dear," said Moominmamma, "I've noticed that! And I should be glad to get rid of you for a bit. Can't you go off to the cave for a few days? It's cooler there, and you can swim and laze all day without disturbing anyone."

"Can we *sleep* in the cave, too?" Moomintroll asked, excitedly.

"Certainly," said Moominmamma. "And don't come home until you're better tempered."

It was very thrilling really to *live* in the cave. In the middle of the sandy floor they put a kerosene lamp, and then everyone dug a hole to fit himself and made a bed in it. The provisions were divided into six big equal portions, which included raisin-pudding and pumpkin jam, bananas, marzipan pigs and sweet maize, and a pancake as well for breakfast next day.

A little breeze came murmuring sadly across the lonely shore, while the sun sank in a red glow filling the cave with its last rays: a reminder of the mysterious darkness that was to come. Then Snufkin played his mouth-organ while the Snork Maiden laid her curly head in Moomintroll's lap, and everyone began to feel comfy inside after the raisin-pudding. And as twilight came stealing into the cave a nice creepy feeling came over them.

Sniff pointed out for the hundredth time that it was he who had found the cave first, but for once nobody bothered to squash him. Then Snufkin lit the lamp and asked, "Shall I tell you something awful?"

The Hemulen immediately wanted to know how awful.

"About as awful as this," said Snufkin, stretching out his arms as wide as possible, "if you see what I mean!"

"No, I don't!" replied the Hemulen. "But go ahead, Snufkin, and I'll tell you when I get frightened."

"Good," said Snufkin. "It's a strange story, and I got it from the Magpie. Well, at the end of the world there lies a mountain so high it makes you dizzy even to think about it. It is as black as soot, as smooth as silk, terribly steep, and where there should be a bottom, there are only clouds. But high up on the peak stands the Hobgoblin's House, and it looks like this." And Snufkin drew a house in the sand.

"Hasn't it got any windows?" asked Sniff.

"No," said Snufkin, "and it hasn't got a door either, because the Hobgoblin always goes home by air, riding on a black panther. He goes out every night and collects rubies in his hat."

"What did you say?" asked Sniff, with his eyes popping out of his head. "Rubies! Where does he get them from?"

"The Hobgoblin can change himself into anything he likes," Snufkin answered, "and then he can crawl

under the ground and even down onto the sea bed
where buried treasure lies."

"What does he do with all those precious stones?"
asked Sniff, enviously.

"Nothing. He just collects them," said Snufkin. "Like the Hemulen collects plants."

"What was that?" asked the Hemulen waking up in his hole.

"I was saying that the Hobgoblin has a whole houseful of rubies," went on Snufkin. "They lie in heaps all over the place and are set into the walls like wild beasts' eyes. The Hobgoblin's House has no roof and the clouds that fly over it are as red as blood with the reflection of the rubies. His eyes are red, too, and they shine in the dark!"

"Now I'm nearly frightened," said the Hemulen. "Do be careful how you go on."

"How happy he must be, this Hobgoblin," exclaimed Sniff.

"He isn't a bit," replied Snufkin, "and he won't be until he finds the King's Ruby. It's almost as big as the black panther's head, and to look into it is like looking at leaping flames. The Hobgoblin has looked for the King's Ruby on all the planets including Neptune—but he hasn't found it. Just now he has gone off to the moon to search in the craters, but he hasn't much hope of success, because in his heart of hearts the Hobgoblin believes that the King's Ruby lies in the sun, where he can never go because it is too hot."

"But is all this true?" asked the Snork's suspicious voice.

"Think what you like," said Snufkin, carelessly, peeling his banana. "Do you know what the Magpie thinks? She thinks that the Hobgoblin had a tall, black hat, a hat that he lost when he went to the moon a couple of months ago."

"You don't mean it!" burst out Moomintroll, and the others made excited noises.

"What's that?" enquired the Hemulen. "What are you talking about?"

"The hat," Sniff told him. "The tall, black hat I found last spring: the Hobgoblin's Hat!" Snufkin nodded, meaningly.

"But suppose he comes back for his hat?" asked a trembling Snork Maiden. "I shall never dare to look at his red eyes."

"We must talk to Mother about this," said Moomintroll. "Is it far to the moon?"

"Quite a distance," answered Snufkin. "Besides, it's sure to take the Hobgoblin a long time to search through all the craters."

There was an anxious silence for a time, while everybody thought about the black hat standing on the chest of drawers under the mirror at home.

"Turn up the lamp a little," quavered Sniff.

Suddenly the Hemulen jumped and said, "Did you hear anything—there, outside?"

They stared toward the black mouth of the cave and listened. Soft pattering sounds—could it be a panther's footsteps!

"It's only the rain," said Moomintroll. "The rain has come at last. Now we'll sleep for a bit."

And they crept into their sandholes and pulled the blankets over them. Moomintroll put out the lamp and, with the rain whispering outside, he floated off to sleep.

The Hemulen woke up with a start. He had been dreaming that he was in a small, leaky boat, and the water had just reached his chin when, to his horror, the dream turned into real life. The rain had come through the roof during the night, and it had drained in absolute torrents into the poor Hemulen's bed.

"Misery me!" he groaned. Then he wrung out his dress and went to look at the weather. It was the same everywhere—grey and wet and miserable. The Hemulen wished he felt like a bath, but he didn't. "Yesterday it was too hot and now it's too wet. I shall go in and lie down again," he said.

The Snork's sandhole looked quite dry.

"Look!" said the Hemulen, "it has rained in my bed."

"Bad luck," said the Snork, and turned over on his other side.

"So I think I shall sleep in your hole," announced the Hemulen. "No snoring now!"

But the Snork only grunted a little and slept on. Then the Hemulen's heart was filled with a desire for revenge, and he dug a trench between his own sand-hole and the Snork's.

"That was most un-Hemulenish!" said the Snork,

sitting up in his wet blanket. "I'm amazed you had
the brains to think of it."

"Well, I'm a bit surprised myself," said the Hemulen. "And now, what shall we do today?"

The Snork stuck his nose out of the mouth of the
cave and looked at the sky and the sea. Then he said
knowingly, "Fishing. Wake up the others while I go
and get the boat in order." And he strolled down
onto the wet sand and out onto the landing stage,
which Moominpappa had built, sniffing the sea air.
It was quite still; the rain was falling softly and each
drop made a ring in the gleaming water. The Snork
nodded to himself, and took out the longest fishing-
line they had. Then he hauled out the landing-net
and baited the hooks while he whistled Snufkin's
hunting song.

Everything was ready when the others came out of
the cave.

"Ah! There you are at last," said the Snork. "Hemul, take down the mast and put in the rowlocks."

"*Must* we fish?" asked the Snork Maiden. "Nothing ever happens when we fish, and I'm so sorry for the little pike."

"Yes, but today something *is* going to happen," said her brother. "You sit in the bow where you'll be least in the way."

"Let me help, too," squeaked Sniff, catching hold of the line. He leapt down onto the edge of the boat, which tipped up, and the line got all tangled with the rowlocks and the anchor.

"Splendid!" said the Snork sarcastically. "Quite splendid. Thoroughly accustomed to the sea. Peace in the boat and all that. Above all respect for other people's work. Ha!"

"Aren't you going to scold him?" the Hemulen asked, incredulously.

"Scold? I?" said the Snork, and laughed mirthlessly. "Has the captain anything to say? Never! Put out the line as it is—it might catch an old boot!" And he retired into the stern and dragged a tarpaulin over his head.

"Goodness gracious me!" said Moomintroll. "You had better take the oars, Snufkin, while we unravel this mess. Sniff, you are a nincompoop."

"I know," said Sniff, glad to have something to do. "Which end shall we begin?"

"In the middle," said Moomintroll. "But don't get your tail tangled up in it too."

And Snufkin slowly rowed *The Adventure* out to sea.

While all this was happening Moominmamma was bustling about feeling very pleased. The rain fell gently on the garden. Peace, order, and quiet reigned everywhere.

"Now everything will grow!" said Moominmamma to herself. And oh! How wonderful to have her family safely away in the cave! She decided to do a bit of tidying up, and began collecting socks, orange peel, Moomintroll's queer stones, bits of bark, and all sorts of odd things. On top of the radio she found some poisonous pink perennials that the Hemulen had forgotten to put into his plant press. Moominmamma twirled them into a ball while she listened thoughtfully to the soft murmur of the rain. "Now everything will grow!" she said once again and without thinking what she was doing she dropped the ball into the Hobgoblin's Hat. Then she went up to her room for a snooze (for Moominmamma dearly loves to snooze while the rain patters on the roof).

Meanwhile in the depths of the sea lay the Snork's long fishing-line . . . waiting. It had already waited two hours and the Snork Maiden was getting desperately impatient.

"Anticipation is the best part," Moomintroll told her. "There might be something on every hook you know." (This fishing-line had lots of hooks.)

The Snork Maiden sighed a little. "Anyway, you know that when you sink the line it has bait on it, and when you haul it up it has a fish—"

"But there might be nothing at all," said Snufkin.

"Or there might be an octopus," said the Hemulen.

"Girls never understand these things," said the Snork. "Now we can begin to pull it up. But nobody must make a sound. Be quiet, everyone."

The first hook came up.

It was empty.

The second hook came up.

It was empty, too.

"It only shows that the fish go deep, and are awfully big," said the Snork. "Quiet now, everybody!"

He pulled up four more empty hooks and said, "This *is* a cunning one. He's eaten up all our bait. Gosh! He must be huge!"

Everybody leaned over the side and peered down into the black depths.

"What sort of fish do you think it is?" asked Sniff.

"A Mameluke at least," said the Snork. "Look! Ten more empty hooks."

"Dear, dear," said the Snork Maiden, sarcastically.

"Dear, dear to you," said her brother, angrily, and went on hauling. "Be quiet—otherwise you'll frighten him away."

Hook after hook came up twisted with seagrass and seaweed. No fish: absolutely nothing at all.

Suddenly the Snork shouted. "Look out! It gave a pull! I'm absolutely sure it gave a pull."

"A Mameluke!" squeaked Sniff.

"Now you *must* keep calm," said the Snork, who felt anything but calm himself. "Dead silence. Here he comes!"

The tight line had suddenly gone limp, but far down in the mysterious green depths gleamed something white. Was it the Mameluke's pale belly? Something huge and terrible seemed to rise up from the strange underwater scene. It was green and mushy like the stem of a great jungle plant, and it slid up under the boat.

"The landing-net!" screamed the Snork. "Where's the landing-net?"

At the same moment the air was filled with noise and flying foam. A terrific wave caught *The Adventure* up on its crest and dashed the fishing line down on the deck. Then suddenly all was still again.

Only the broken line dangled sadly over the side, and a huge whirl in the water marked where the monster had passed.

"*Now* who said it was a pike?" the Snork asked his sister, bitterly. "I shall *never* get over this as long as I live!"

"This is where it broke," said the Hemulen holding up the line. "Something told me it was too thin."

"Oh, do shut up," said the Snork, and hid his face in his paws.

The Hemulen wanted to say something, but Snufkin kicked him on the shins. They all sat in hopeless silence. Then the Snork Maiden said, rather timidly, "What do you think about having another try? We could use the painter for a line."

The Snork grunted. After a while he said, "And what about the hooks?"

"Your pocketknife," said the Snork Maiden. "If you open the blade *and* the corkscrew *and* the screwdriver *and* the instrument-for-taking-stones-out-of-horses'-hooves, he's sure to catch onto something."

The Snork took his paws away from his eyes and said, "Yes, but we haven't any bait?"

"Pancake," said his sister.

The Snork considered this for a time, while they all held their breath with excitement.

At last he said, "Of course if the Mameluke eats pancake, then . . ." And everyone knew that the hunt would go on.

They tied the pocketknife firmly to the painter

with a bit of wire that the Hemulen had in his skirt-pocket, they stuck the pancake on the knife, and dropped the whole lot overboard.

Now the Snork Maiden's blood was up and she was as excited as the others.

"You are like Diana," said Moomintroll, admiringly.

"Who's that?" she asked.

"Goddess of the chase!" he replied. "As beautiful as the Wooden Queen and as clever as you!"

"Hm," said the Snork Maiden.

At that moment *The Adventure* keeled over a little.

"Hush!" said the Snork. "He's nibbling!" There was another twitch—this time more violent—and then came a furious jerk that knocked them all over.

"Help!" screamed Sniff. "He's going to gobble us up!"

The Adventure's bows dipped alarmingly, but she righted herself again and set off at a terrific speed towards the open sea. The painter was stretched out, tight as a bowstring, in front of her and disappeared in a flurry of foam below the surface.

The Mameluke obviously liked pancake!

"Keep calm!" yelled the Snork. "Calm in the boat! Every man to his post!"

"As long as he doesn't dive . . ." thought Snufkin creeping into the bows.

But the Mameluke set a course straight out to sea, and soon the shore lay, like the sweep of a paint-brush, far behind them.

"How long do you think he will be able to hold on?" asked the Hemulen.

"If the worst comes to the worst we can cut the line," said Sniff.

"Never," declared the Snork Maiden, shaking her curly fringe.

And then the Mameluke gave his huge tail a whisk and swung around, making for the coast again.

"He's going a little slower now," shouted Moomintroll, who was on his knees in the bows. "He's beginning to get tired!"

The Mameluke *was* tired, but he had also begun to get angry. He gave the line a jerk and then tore off again so that *The Adventure* rocked about in the most alarming way.

Sometimes he lay quite still trying to fool them, and then suddenly he would set off with such speed that a tidal wave almost swamped them. So Snufkin took his mouth-organ and played his hunting song, while the others beat time with so much energy that the deck shook. And then, when they had almost given up hope, the Mameluke floated over on his back turning his huge lifeless belly up to the light.

They had never seen such a big fish! They contemplated it for a moment in silence and then the Snork said, "Well, I got him at last, didn't I?" And his sister proudly agreed.

While the Mameluke was being towed to land it

began to rain, and soon the Hemulen's dress got soaked through, and Snufkin's hat lost what was left of its shape—which wasn't much.

"It'll probably be pretty wet in the cave now," said Moomintroll, who sat freezing at the oars.

"Mother may be worried," he added after a while.

"You mean that we could sort of go home soon?" said Sniff, trying not to sound too hopeful.

"Yes, and show them the fish," said the Snork.

"We *will* go home," said the Hemulen. "Strange adventures, and getting wet, and carrying on alone and that sort of thing are all very well, but they're not comfortable in the long run."

So they put boards under the Mameluke and everyone helped to carry him through the wood. His wide-open mouth was so big that the branches caught in his teeth, and he weighed so many hundreds of pounds that they had to rest every few minutes. Meanwhile, the rain got worse and worse, until, when they got to their valley, it hid the whole house.

"What about leaving him here for a bit?" suggested Sniff.

"Not on your life!" said Moomintroll, indignantly, and they plunged on through the garden. Suddenly the Snork stood stock still. "We've come the wrong way!" he said.

"Nonsense!" said Moomintroll. "Isn't that the woodshed? And down there's the bridge."

"Yes, but where's the house?" asked the Snork.

It was most extraordinary. Moominhouse had

vanished. Quite simply—it wasn't there. They laid down the Mameluke in front of the steps—at least that is to say—where the steps ought to have been. Instead . . .

But first I must explain what had happened in the Valley while they were out on the Mameluke Hunt.

Moominmamma had gone upstairs for a snooze, but before doing so she had dropped the ball of poisonous pink perennials into the Hobgoblin's Hat in an absentminded moment. The trouble was she should never have tidied up really, for while the house lay deep in its after-lunch nap, the ball of poisonous pink perennials began to grow in a strange and bewitched fashion. It twisted slowly up out of the hat, and crept down onto the floor. Tendrils and shoots groped their way up the walls, clambered round the curtains and blind-cords, and scrambled through the cracks, ventilators, and keyholes. In the damp air flowers came out and fruit began to ripen, and huge leafy shoots blotted out the stairs, pushed their way between the legs of the furniture, and hung in festoons from the chandelier.

The house was filled with a soft rustling sound: sometimes the pop of an opening bud could be heard, or the thud of ripe fruit falling on the carpet. But Moominmamma thought it was only the rain and turned over on her other side and went to sleep again.

In the next room Moominpappa sat writing his memoirs. Nothing amusing had happened since he had built the landing stage, so he went on with the

101

story of his childhood, and this brought such memories that he nearly burst into tears. He had always been a bit out of the ordinary as a child, and nobody had ever understood him. When he got older it was the same, and he had had a frightful time in every way. Moominpappa wrote and wrote thinking how sorry everyone would be when they read his story, and this cheered him up again, and he said to himself, "It will serve them jolly well right!"

Just then a ripe plum fell onto his paper and made a big, sticky blot.

"Bless my tail!" burst out Moominpappa. "Moomintroll and Sniff must be home again!" And he turned round to scold them. But nobody was behind him: instead he found himself staring at a thick bush covered with yellow berries. He jumped up, and at once blue plums rained down on him from every side. Then he noticed that a great branch was growing slowly towards the window with green shoots sprouting out in all directions.

"Hullo!" yelled Moominpappa. "Wake up, everybody! Come quickly!"

Moominmamma woke up with a start, and, to her amazement, saw that her room was full of small, white flowers, hanging down from the ceiling in leafy garlands.

"Oh, how beautiful!" she said. "Moomintroll must have done this as a surprise for me." And she carefully drew aside the thin curtain of flowers by her bed and stepped onto the floor.

"Hullo!" Moominpappa was still yelling on the other side of the wall. "Open the door! I can't get out!"

But Moominmamma couldn't open the door into his room because it was completely overgrown with creepers. So she broke a pane of glass in her own door and, with enormous difficulty, squeezed through onto the landing. There was a small forest on the staircase, and the drawing room was a positive jungle.

"Dear me!" said Moominmamma. "Of course it's that hat again." And she sat down and fanned herself with a palm-leaf.

And the shoots grew up through the chimneys and climbed down over the roof, covering the whole of Moominhouse with a thick green carpet, while out in the rain Moomintroll stood and stared at the big, green mound where the flowers went on opening their petals and the fruit ripened from green to yellow, from yellow to red.

"It used to be here anyhow," said Sniff.

"It's inside," said Moomintroll miserably. "But *we* can't get in and *they* can't get out."

Snufkin went off to explore the green mound; there was no window or door: only a dense wild mass of vegetation. He took hold of a creeper which turned out to be as tough as rubber and impossible to move, but as he went by it threw a loop, as if on purpose, round his hat and lifted it right off his head.

"More hobgoblinery," muttered Snufkin. "It's beginning to get tiresome."

Meanwhile Sniff ran across the overgrown verandah and, with a delighted squeak, discovered that the door to the cellar was still open. Moomintroll hurried after him and peered in through the black hole. "In with you all!" he said. "But hurry up before it gets overgrown here, too," and they crawled into the dark cellar, one after another.

"Hi!" shouted the Hemulen who was last. "I can't get through."

"Then you can stay outside and guard the Mameluke," said the Snork. "You can botanize on the house now, can't you?"

And while the poor Hemulen whimpered outside in the rain, the others groped their way up the cellar steps.

"We're in luck," said Moomintroll when he reached the top. "The door's open. It pays to be careless sometimes."

"I'm the culprit," squeaked Sniff. "So you can thank me!"

As they pushed through the door a remarkable sight met their eyes: the Muskrat was sitting in the fork of a tree eating a pear.

"Where's Mother?" asked Moomintroll.

"She's trying to get your father out of his room," replied the Muskrat, bitterly. "This is what comes of collecting plants. I've never quite trusted that Hemulen. Well, I hope the Muskrat heaven is a peaceful place, because I shan't be *here* much longer."

They listened for a moment to the sound of enormous axe blows coming from upstairs. Then came a crash and a whoop of joy. Moominpappa was free!

"Mamma! Pappa!" shouted Moomintroll, pushing his way through the jungle to the bottom of the stairs. "What *have* you been doing while I was away?"

"Well, dear," replied Moominmamma. "We must have been careless with the Hobgoblin's Hat again. But come up here—I've found a gooseberry bush in the wardrobe."

It was a thrilling afternoon. They played a jungle game in which Moomintroll was Tarzan and the Snork Maiden was Jane. Sniff was Tarzan's Son, and Snufkin was the chimpanzee Cheetah, while the Snork crawled about in the undergrowth, with huge teeth made of orange-peel,* pretending to be the Enemy.

---

*Ask your mother how to make them: she will know. *Author.*

"Now I shall steal Jane away," he cried, dragging the Snork Maiden by the tail to a hole under the dining-room table, so that Moomintroll, when he came home to their house in the chandelier, and discovered what had happened, had to lower himself to the ground on a creeper and dash off to the rescue. Then he produced a Tarzan roar from the top of the airing cupboard, and Jane and the rest of them roared back.

"Well, things can't get much worse—that's one consolation," the Muskrat groaned. He had hidden himself in a forest of bracken in the bathroom, and had wrapped his head in a handkerchief so that nothing should grow into his ears.

But Moominmamma was quite unperturbed. "Well, well!" she said, "it seems to me that our guests are having a very good time."

"I hope so," replied Moominpappa. "Pass me a banana, please, dear."

And so it went on until the evening. Nobody bothered about whether the cellar door was getting overgrown, and nobody even thought about the poor Hemulen. He still sat, with his wet dress flapping round his legs, guarding the Mameluke. Sometimes he ate an apple or counted the stamens in a jungle flower, but in between he mostly sighed.

It had stopped raining, and night began to fall. And at the moment that the sun went down something happened to the green mound that was Moominhouse: it began to wither as quickly as it

had grown; the fruit shriveled and fell to the ground; the flowers drooped and the leaves curled up, and once more the house was filled with rustlings and cracklings.

The Hemulen watched for a bit, and then he went and pulled gently at a branch. It came off at once and was as dry as tinder. Then the Hemulen had an idea. He collected a huge pile of sticks and branches, went to the woodshed for matches, and then lit a crackling bonfire in the middle of the garden path.

Pleased and happy, he sat himself down beside the blaze to dry his dress, and after a while he had another idea. With super-Hemulenish strength he dragged the Mameluke's tail into the fire. Roasted fish was the best thing he had ever tasted.

Thus it was that when the Moomin family and

108

their friends pushed their way through the verandah and burst the door open, they found a very happy Hemulen who had already eaten up one seventh of the Mameluke.

"You wretch!" said the Snork. "How can I weigh my fish now?"

"Weigh *me* and add it on," suggested the Hemulen. It was one of his brighter days.

"Now we'll burn up the jungle," said Moominpappa. And they carried out all the rubbish from the house and made a bigger bonfire than anyone had ever seen in the valley before.

The Mameluke was roasted whole in the embers and eaten up from tip to tail. But long afterward there were quarrels about how long he had been: had he stretched from the bottom of the verandah steps to the woodshed, or only as far as the lilac bushes?

Chapter 6

*In which Thingumy and Bob, bringing a
mysterious suitcase and followed by the Groke,
come into the story, and in which the Snork
leads a Court Case.*

Early one morning at the beginning of August
Thingumy and Bob came walking over the mountain, and stopped just where Sniff had found the
Hobgoblin's Hat. Thingumy wore a red cap and Bob
carried an enormous suitcase. They had come a very
long way and were rather tired, so they rested for a
bit and looked down over the Valley of the Moomins,
where the smoke from Moominhouse was rising between the silver poplars and plum trees.

"Smoke," said Thingumy.

"Foke means smood," said Bob nodding. And they began to wander down to the valley talking in the strange way that Thingumies and Bobs do talk. (It isn't clear to everyone, but the main thing is that they understand each other.)

Very cautiously they tiptoed up to the house and stood shyly by the front steps. "Do you think we could go in?" asked Thingumy. "It depends," said Bob. "Don't be frightened if they're gross and crumpy."

"Shall we dock on the knoor?" suggested Thingumy. "But imagine if somebody comes out and screams!"

Just then Moominmamma stuck her head out of the window and shouted, "Coffee!"

Thingumy and Bob were so dreadfully frightened that they jumped into the opening of the potato-cellar.

"Oh!" said Moominmamma with a start, "I believe those were mice disappearing into the cellar. Sniff, run down with a little milk for them." Then she caught sight of the suitcase which stood by the steps. "Luggage, too," thought Moominmamma. "Dear me—then they've come to stay." And she went off to look for Moominpappa to ask him to put up two more beds—very, very small ones. Meanwhile Thingumy and Bob had dug themselves into the potatoes so that only their eyes could be seen, and there they waited in terror for what might happen to them.

"Anyway I can fell smood," muttered Thingumy.

"Somebody's coming," whispered Bob. "Sot a nound!"

The cellar door creaked and at the top of the steps stood Sniff with a lantern in one paw and a saucer of milk in the other.

"Hi! Where are you?" he shouted.

Thingumy and Bob crept still farther down and held on to each other tight.

"Will you have some milk?" said Sniff.

"Don't nake any totice," whispered Bob.

"If you think I'm going to stand here half the day," said Sniff angrily, "you're mistaken. I suppose you don't know any better. Silly old mice who haven't the sense to come in by the front door!"

"Milly old souse yourself!" retorted Thingumy and Bob, who were seriously upset by this.

"Oh! So they're foreigners," thought Sniff. "I'd better fetch Moominmamma." And he locked the cellar door and ran into the kitchen.

"Well? Did they like the milk?" Moominmamma asked.

"They talk a foreign language," said Sniff. "Nobody can understand what they say."

"What's it like?" asked Moomintroll, who was shelling peas with the Hemulen.

" 'Milly old souse yourself'!" said Sniff.

Moominmamma sighed. "This is going to be a nice mix-up," she said. "How shall I be able to find out what they want for pudding on their birthday, or how many pillows they like to have?"

"We'll soon learn their language," said Moomintroll. "It sounds easy."

"I think I understand them," said the Hemulen reflectively. "Didn't they tell Sniff he was a silly old mouse?"

Sniff blushed and tossed his head.

"Go and talk to them yourself if you're so clever," he said.

So the Hemulen lumbered away to the cellar steps and called out kindly, "Welcome to Hoomin-mouse!"

Thingumy and Bob stuck their heads out of the potato pile and looked at him.

"Mere's some hilk," continued the Hemulen.

Then they scampered up the steps and into the drawing room.

Sniff looked at them and noticed that they were much smaller than he was, so he felt kinder and said, condescendingly, "Hullo. Nice to see you."

"Thanks. Yame to sou," said Thingumy.

"Did I fell smood?" enquired Bob.

"What do they say now?" asked Moominmamma.

"They're hungry," said the Hemulen. "But they still don't seem to take to Sniff."

"Give them my compliments then," said Sniff, hotly, "and say that never in my life have I seen two such fish-faces. And now I'm going out."

"Piff is sneevish," said the Hemulen. "Nake no totice."

"Anyway come in and have some coffee," said Moominmamma nervously, and she showed Thingumy and Bob out onto the verandah. The Hemulen, who was very proud of his new rank as interpreter, followed them.

And that was how Thingumy and Bob came to live at Moominhouse. They didn't make much noise, spent most of the time hand-in-hand, and never lost sight of their suitcase. But toward dusk on that first day they began to get very worried: they ran frantically up and down stairs several times, and eventually hid under the drawing-room carpet.

"Mot's the watter?" asked the Hemulen.

"The Groke is coming!" whispered Bob.

"Groke? Who's that?" asked the Hemulen, getting a bit frightened.

"Tig and brim and gerrible!" said Bob. "Lock the door against her."

The Hemulen ran to Moominmamma and told her the awful news.

"They say that a big and grim and terrible Groke is coming here. We must lock all the doors tonight."

"But I don't think any of the doors have keys, except the cellar," said Moominmamma in a worried voice. "Dear me! It's always the same with newcomers." And she went to talk to Moominpappa about it.

"We must arm ourselves and move the furniture in front of the door," declared Moominpappa. "A large Groke like that may be dangerous. I shall set an alarm clock in the drawing room, and Thingumy and Bob can sleep under my bed."

But Thingumy and Bob had already crept into a bureau drawer and refused to come out.

Moominpappa shook his head and went to the woodshed for his blunderbuss.

The evenings were already beginning to draw in; the glowworms were out with their little torches, and the garden was filled with black, velvet shadows. The wind soughed drearily through the trees, and Moominpappa felt an uncanny feeling creeping over him as he went down the path. Suppose this Groke were hiding behind a bush! What did she look like, and above all, how big was she? When he came in again he put the sofa in front of the door and said, "We must leave the light on all night. You must all be on the alert and Snufkin must sleep indoors." It was terribly exciting . . . Then he knocked on the bureau drawer and said, "We shall protect you!" But there was no answer, so he pulled the drawer out to see if Thingumy and Bob had already been kidnapped. However, they slept peacefully, and beside them lay their suitcase.

"Anyway, let's go to bed," said Moominpappa. "But arm yourselves, all of you."

With much noise and chatter they went off to their rooms and presently silence reigned in Moominhouse, while the solitary kerosene lamp burned on the drawing-room table.

It was midnight. Then one o'clock struck. A little after two the Muskrat woke up and wanted to get out of bed. He staggered sleepily downstairs and stopped in amazement in front of the sofa which stood across the door. "What an idea!" he muttered, trying to drag it away, and then of course the alarm clock that Moominpappa had put there started ringing.

In a moment the house was filled with screams, shots, and the stamping of feet, as everybody came rushing down to the drawing room armed with axes, spades, rakes, stones, knives, and scissors, and stood staring at the Muskrat.

"Where's the Groke?" demanded Moomintroll.

"Oh, it was only me," said the Muskrat peevishly. "I just wanted to look at the stars. I forgot all about your stupid Groke."

"Then go outside at once," said Moomintroll. "But don't do it again." And he threw the door open.

Then—they saw the Groke. Everybody saw her. She sat motionless on the sandy path at the bottom of the steps and stared at them with round, expressionless eyes.

She was not particularly big and didn't look dangerous either, but you felt that she was terribly evil and would wait for ever. And *that* was awful.

Nobody plucked up enough courage to attack. She sat there for a while, and then slid away into the darkness. But where she had been sitting the ground was frozen!

The Snork shut the door and shook himself. "Poor

Thingumy and Bob!" he said. "Hemul, look and see
if they're awake."

They were.

"Has she gone?" asked Thingumy.

"Yes, you can peep in sleace now," replied the
Hemulen.

Thingumy sighed a little and said, "Thank goodness!" And they pulled the suitcase with them as far
into the drawer as possible and went to sleep again.

"Can we go back to bed now?" asked Moominmamma, putting down her axe.

"Yes, Mother," said Moomintroll. "Snufkin and I
will stand guard till the sun gets up. But put your
handbag under your pillow to be on the safe side."

Then they sat alone in the drawing room and played poker till the morning. And no more was heard of the Groke that night.

Next morning the Hemulen went anxiously out to the kitchen and said, "I've been talking to Thingumy and Bob."

"Well, what is it now?" asked Moominamma with a sigh.

"It's their suitcase the Groke wants," explained the Hemulen.

"What a monster!" burst out Moominmamma. "To steal their small possessions from them!"

"Yes, I know," said the Hemulen, "but there is something that makes the whole thing complicated. It seems to be the Groke's suitcase."

"Hm," agreed Moominmamma. "That certainly makes the situation more difficult. We'll talk to the Snork. He always arranges everything so well."

The Snork was very interested. "It's a remarkable case," he said. "We must hold a meeting. Everybody will come to the lilac bushes at three o'clock to discuss the question."

It was one of those lovely warm afternoons full of the scent of flowers and the humming of bees, and the garden was brilliant with the deep colors of late summer.

The Muskrat's hammock was hung between two bushes and on it was a notice which said:

PROSECUTOR for the GROKE

The Snork himself, in a wig, was sitting in front of a box: everybody could see that he was the judge. Opposite him sat Thingumy and Bob eating cherries in the prisoners' dock.

"I wish to be their Prosecutor," said Sniff (who hadn't forgotten that they had called him a silly old mouse).

"In that case I'll be their Counsel for the Defense," said the Hemulen.

"What about me?" asked the Snork Maiden.

"You can be the Moomin Family's witness," said her brother. "And Snufkin can make notes concerning the proceedings of the Court. But you're to do it properly, Snufkin!"

"Why doesn't the Groke have a Counsel for the Defense?" asked Sniff.

"That isn't necessary," replied the Snork, "because the Groke is in the right. Everything clear now? All right. We'll begin."

He banged three times on the box with a hammer.

"Man you cake it out?" asked Thingumy.

"Mot nutch," said Bob, blowing a cherry stone at the judge.

"You are not to speak until I say so," said the Snork. "Yes or No. Nothing more. Is the said suitcase yours or the Groke's?"

"Yes," said Thingumy.

"No," said Bob.

"Write down that they contradicted each other," screamed Sniff.

The Snork banged on the box. "Quiet!" he cried. "Now I'm asking for the last time. Whose suitcase is it?"

"Ours!" said Thingumy.

"Now they say it's theirs," moaned the Hemulen, in despair, "and this morning they said the opposite."

"Well, then we don't have to give it to the Groke," said the Snork with a sigh of relief. "But it's a pity after all my arrangements."

Thingumy leaned forward and whispered something to the Hemulen. "They say," he declared, "that it's only the *Contents* of the suitcase that belongs to the Groke."

"Ha!" said Sniff. "I can well believe that. Now

everything is perfectly clear. The Groke gets her Contents back and the fish-faces keep their old suit-case."

"It's not clear at all!" cried the Hemulen boldly. "The question is not who is the *owner* of the Contents, but who has the greatest *right* to the Contents. The right thing in the right place. You saw the Groke, everybody? Now, I ask you, did she look as if she had a right to the Contents?"

"That's true enough," said Sniff in surprise. "Clever of you, Hemul. But, on the other hand, think how lonely the Groke is because nobody likes her, and she hates everybody. The Contents is perhaps the only thing she has. Would you now take that away from her too—lonely and rejected in the night?" Sniff became more and more affected and his voice trembled. "Cheated out of her only possession by Thingumy and Bob." He blew his nose and couldn't go on.

The Snork banged the box. "The Groke doesn't need any defense," he said. "Besides, your point of view is emotional, and so is the Hemulen's. Witness forward! Speak up!"

"We like Thingumy and Bob very much," said the Moomin Family's witness. "We disapproved of the Groke from the beginning. It's a pity if she must have her Contents back."

"Right is right," said the Snork, solemnly. "You must be fair. Particularly as Thingumy and Bob can't see the difference between right and wrong. They were born like that and can't help it. Prosecutor, what have you to say?"

But the Muskrat had gone to sleep in his hammock.

"Well, well," said the Snork. "I'm sure he wasn't interested anyway. Have we said all we should say before I pronounce the verdict?"

"Excuse me," said the Moomin Family's witness, "but wouldn't it be easier if we knew what the Contents actually are?"

Thingumy whispered something again. The Hemulen nodded. "It's a secret," he said. "Thingumy and Bob think the Contents is the most beautiful thing in the world, but the Groke just thinks it's the most expensive."

The Snork nodded many times and wrinkled his forehead. "This is a difficult case," he said. "Thingumy and Bob have reasoned correctly, but they have acted wrongly. Right is right. I must think. Quiet now!"

It was quite quiet amongst the lilac bushes except for the humming of the bees, while the garden baked in the sunshine.

Suddenly a cold breeze swept over the grass. The sun went behind a cloud and the garden looked dull.

"What was that?" said Snufkin and lifted his pen from the notes.

"She's here again," whispered the Snork Maiden.

In the frozen grass sat the Groke, glaring at them.

She fixed her gaze on Thingumy and Bob, began growling, and shambled slowly nearer.

"Hopster! Hopster! Help! Help! Stopster!" they screamed, getting quite incoherent in their terror.

"Stop, Groke!" said the Snork. "I have something to say to you!"

The Groke stopped.

"I have thought enough," went on the Snork. "Will you agree to Thingumy and Bob buying the Contents of the suitcase? And if so what is your price?"

"High," said the Groke in an icy voice.

"Would my gold mountain on the Hattifatteners' Island be enough?" asked the Snork.

"No," answered the Groke as icily as before.

But just then Moominmamma noticed how cold it had got, and she decided to fetch her shawl. So she ran through the garden, where the frost marked the Groke's tracks, and up onto the verandah. And there she had an idea. Picking up the Hobgoblin's Hat she went back to the Court proceedings, put the hat on the grass and said, "Here is the most valuable thing in the whole of Moomin Valley, Groke! Do you know what has grown out of this hat? Raspberry juice and fruit trees, and the most beautiful little self-propelling clouds: the only Hobgoblin's Hat in the world!"

"Show!" said the Groke scornfully.

Then Moominmamma laid a few cherries in the hat, and everybody waited in dead silence.

"If only they don't turn into something nasty,"

whispered Snufkin to the Hemulen. But they were in luck. When the Groke looked into the hat a handful of red rubies lay there.

"There," said Moominmamma happily, "and think what would happen if you put a pumpkin in it!"

The Groke looked at the hat. Then she looked at Thingumy and Bob. Then she looked at the hat again. You could see that she was thinking with all her might. Then suddenly she snatched the hat and, without a word, slithered like an icy grey shadow into the forest. It was the last time she was seen in the Valley of the Moomins, and the last they saw of the Hobgoblin's Hat, too.

At once the colors became warmer again and the garden was filled with the sounds and scents of summer.

"Thank goodness we've got rid of that hat," said Moominmamma. "Now it's done something sensible for once."

"But the clouds *were* fun," said Sniff.

"And playing Tarzan in the jungle," added Moomintroll sadly.

"Rood giddance to rad bubbish!" said Thingumy taking the suitcase in one hand and Bob in the other, and together they walked off toward Moominhouse while the others stood looking after them.

"What do they say now?" asked Sniff.

"Well! 'Good afternoon!' is near enough," said the Hemulen.

Chapter 7

*Which is very long and describes Snufkin's
departure and how the Contents of the
mysterious suitcase were revealed; also how
Moominmamma found her handbag and
arranged a party to celebrate it, and
finally how the Hobgoblin arrived
in the Valley of the Moomins.*

It was the end of August—the time when owls hoot
at night and flurries of bats swoop noiselessly over
the garden. Moomin Wood was full of glowworms,
and the sea was disturbed. There was expectation
and a certain sadness in the air, and the harvest
moon came up huge and yellow. Moomintroll had

always liked those last weeks of summer most, but he didn't really know why.

The wind and the sea had changed their tone; there was a new feeling in the air; the trees stood waiting, and Moomintroll wondered if something strange were going to happen. He had woken up and lay looking at the ceiling thinking about the sunshine, and that it must be quite early in the morning.

Then he turned his head and saw that Snufkin's bed was empty. And at that moment he heard the secret signal under his window—a long whistle and two short ones, which meant: "What are your plans for today?"

Moomintroll jumped out of bed and looked out of the window. The sun hadn't reached the garden yet, and it looked cool and enticing down there. Snufkin was waiting.

"Pee-Hoo," said Moomintroll, very quietly so as not to wake anybody, and then he clambered down the rope ladder.

They said "hullo" to each other and then wandered down to the river and sat on the bridge with their legs dangling over the water. The sun had risen above the treetops by this time, and it shone right into their eyes.

"We sat just like this in the spring," said Moomintroll. "Do you remember, we had woken up from our winter sleep and it was the very first day? All the others were still asleep."

Snufkin nodded. He was busy making reed boats and sailing them down the river.

"Where are they going?" asked Moomintroll.

"To places where I'm not," Snufkin answered as, one after another, the little boats swirled away round the bend of the river and disappeared.

"Loaded with cinnamon, sharks' teeth, and emeralds," said Moomintroll.

"You talked of plans," he went on. "Have you got any yourself?"

"Yes," said Snufkin. "I have a plan. But it's a lonely one, you know."

Moomintroll looked at him for a long time, and then he said, "You're thinking of going away."

Snufkin nodded, and they sat for a while swinging their legs over the water, without speaking, while the river flowed on and on beneath them to all the strange places that Snufkin longed for and would go to quite alone.

"When are you going?" Moomintroll asked.

"Now—immediately!" said Snufkin throwing all the reed-boats into the water at once, and he jumped down from the bridge and sniffed the morning air. It was a good day to start a journey; the crest of the hill beckoned to him in the sunshine, with the road winding up and disappearing on the other side to find a new valley, and then a new hill . . .

Moomintroll stood looking on while Snufkin packed up his tent. "Are you staying away long?" he asked.

"No," said Snufkin, "on the first day of spring I shall be here again whistling under your window—a year goes by so quickly!"

"Yes," said Moomintroll. "Cheerio then!"

"So long!" said Snufkin.

Moomintroll was left alone on the bridge. He watched Snufkin grow smaller and smaller, and at last disappear among the silver poplars and the plum trees. But after a while he heard the mouth-organ playing "All small beasts should have bows in their tails," and then he knew that his friend was happy. He waited while the music grew fainter and fainter, till at last it was quite quiet, and then he trotted back through the dewy garden.

On the verandah steps he found Thingumy and Bob curled up in the sunshine.

"Good morning, Troominmoll," said Thingumy.

"Good morning Bingumy and Thob," answered Moomintroll, who had now mastered Thingumy and Bob's strange language.

"Are you crying?" asked Bob.

"N-no," said Moomintroll, "it's only that Snufkin has gone away."

"Oh, dear—pot a wity!" said Thingumy, sympathetically. "Would it cheer you up to niss Bob on the kose?"

So Moomintroll kissed Bob kindly on the nose, but it didn't make him feel any happier.

Then they put their heads together and whispered

for a long time, and at last Bob announced, solemnly, "We've decided to show you the Contents."

"Of the suitcase?" asked Moomintroll.

Thingumy and Bob nodded eagerly. "Come with us!" they said and scuttled away under the hedge.

Moomintroll crawled after them and discovered they had made a secret hiding place in the thickest part of the shrubbery. They had padded it with swansdown and decorated it with shells and small white stones. It was rather dark in there, and nobody passing the hedge would have suspected that there was a secret hiding place on the other side. On a straw mat stood Thingumy and Bob's suitcase.

"That's the Snork Maiden's mat," observed Moomintroll. "She was looking for it only yesterday."

"Oh, yes," agreed Bob, happily. "*We* found it—but she doesn't know, of course."

"Hm," said Moomintroll. "And now weren't you going to show me what you've got in your suitcase?"

They nodded delightedly, and standing on either side of the suitcase said solemnly, "Geady, steady, ro!"

And then the lid opened with a snap.

"Goodness gracious me!" exclaimed Moomintroll. A soft red light lit up the whole place, and before him lay a ruby as big as a panther's head, glowing like the sunset, like living fire.

"Do you like it mery vutch?" asked Thingumy.

"Yes," said Moomintroll faintly.

"And now you won't cry anymore, will you?" said Bob.

Moomintroll shook his head.

Thingumy and Bob sighed contentedly and settled down to contemplate the precious stone. They stared in silent rapture at it.

The ruby changed color all the time. At first it was quite pale, and then suddenly a pink glow would flow over it like the sunrise on a snow-capped mountain—and then again crimson flames shot out of its heart and it seemed like a great black tulip with stamens of fire.

"Oh! If only Snufkin could see it!" sighed Moomintroll, and he stood there a long long time while time grew weary and his thoughts were very big.

At last he said, "It was wonderful. May I come back and look at it another day?"

But Thingumy and Bob didn't answer, so he crawled under the hedge again, feeling a bit giddy in the pale daylight, and had to sit on the grass for a while to recover himself.

"Goodness gracious me!" he repeated. "I'll eat my tail if that isn't the King's Ruby that the Hobgoblin is still looking for in the craters of the moon. To think that this odd little couple have had it in their suitcase all the time!" Just then the Snork Maiden wandered out into the garden and came to sit beside him, but Moomintroll was so sunk in thought that he didn't notice her. After a while she poked cautiously at the tuft of his tail.

"Oh—it's you, is it?" said Moomintroll, jumping up. The Snork Maiden smiled coyly. "Have you seen my hair?" she asked patting her head.

"All right, let's," said Moomintroll absently.

"What *is* the matter with you?" she asked.

"My dear little rose petal, I can't explain, even to you. But my heart is very heavy. You see, Snufkin has gone away."

"Oh, no!" said the Snork Maiden.

"Yes, really. But he did say good-bye to me first," Moomintroll replied. "He didn't wake anyone else."

They sat there on the grass for a while, the sun gradually warming their backs, and then Sniff and the Snork came out on the steps.

"Hullo," said the Snork Maiden. "Do you know that Snufkin has gone south?"

"What, without me?" said Sniff, indignantly.

"One must be alone sometimes," said Moomintroll, "but you're still too young to understand that. Where are the others?"

"The Hemulen has gone to pick mushrooms," said the Snork, "and the Muskrat has taken his hammock in, because he thinks the nights are beginning to get cold. And then your mother is in a very bad mood today."

"Angry or sad?" Moomintroll asked, in surprise.

"More sad I think," answered the Snork.

"Then I must go in to her at once," said Moomintroll. He found Moominmamma sitting on the drawing-room sofa looking most unhappy.

"What is it, Mother?" he asked.

"My dear, something terrible has happened," she said. "My handbag has disappeared. I can't do anything without it. I've searched everywhere, but it isn't there."

So Moomintroll organized a hunt in which everybody but the Muskrat took part. "Of all unnecessary things," said he, "your mother's bag is the most unnecessary. After all time passes and the days change exactly the same whether she has her bag or not."

"That is not the point," said Moominpappa, indignantly. "I must confess that I feel most strangely toward Moominmamma without her bag. I've never seen her without it before!"

"Was there much in it?" asked the Snork.

"No," said Moominmamma, "only things that we might need in a hurry, like dry socks and sweets and string and tummy-powder and so on."

"What reward do we get if we find it?" Sniff wanted to know.

"Almost anything!" said Moominmamma. "I know, I'll give a big party for you, and you can have nothing but cake for tea, and nobody need wash or go to bed early!"

After that the search continued twice as hard. They hunted through the whole house. They looked under the carpets and under the beds; in the stove and in the cellar; in the attic and on the roof. They searched the whole garden, the woodshed and down by the river. The bag was not to be found.

"Perhaps you climbed a tree with it or took it with you when you went to have a bath?" asked Sniff.

But Moominmamma only shook her head and wailed, "Oh, unhappy day!"

Then the Snork suggested putting an advertisement in the paper, which they did, and the paper came out with two big items of news on the front page:

SNUFKIN LEAVES MOOMINDALE
Mysterious departure at dawn.

and in slightly bigger letters:

MOOMINMAMMA'S HANDBAG DISAPPEARS
No clues.
Search in progress.
Biggest-ever August party as reward to finder.

As soon as the news had got about, a huge crowd collected in the wood, on the hills, and by the sea, and even the smallest forest rat joined in the hunt. Only the old and infirm stayed at home, and the whole valley echoed with shouting and running.

"Dear me!" said Moominmamma. "What an up-heaval!" But she was secretly rather pleased about it.

"What's all the buss afout?" asked Thingumy.

"My handbag, of course, dear!" said Moomin-mamma.

"Your black one?" asked Thingumy. "That you can see yourself in, and that has pour fittle lockets?"

"What did you say?" asked Moominmamma, who was far too excited to listen to them.

"The black one with pour fockets?" repeated Thingumy.

"Yes, yes," said Moominmamma. "Run out and play, dears, and don't worry me now."

"What do you think?" asked Bob when they got into the garden.

134

"I can't bear to see her so miserable," said Thingumy.

"I suppose we must bake it tack," said Bob with a sigh. "Pot a wity! It was so nice to sleep in the pittle lockets."

So Thingumy and Bob went to their secret hiding place, which nobody had discovered yet, and pulled Moominmamma's bag out of a rose tree. It was exactly twelve o'clock when they went through the garden dragging the bag between them. The hawk caught sight of the little cavalcade, and went off at once to spread the news over Moomin Valley, and soon the newspaper headlines announced:

MOOMINMAMMA'S HANDBAG FOUND
By Thingumy and Bob.
Touching scenes in Moominhouse.

"Is it really true?" Moominmamma burst out. "Oh, how wonderful! Where did you find it?"

"In a trose ree," began Thingumy. "It was so nice to sleep . . ."

But just then lots of people came rushing in to congratulate them and Moominmamma never found out that her bag had been used as a bedroom by Thingumy and Bob. (And perhaps that was just as well.)

After that nobody could think of anything but the big August party which was to be held that night, and everything had to be gotten ready before the moon rose. How nice it is to prepare for a party that you *know* will be fun, and to which all the right people are coming! Even the Muskrat showed some interest.

"You should have a lot of tables," he said. "Little tables and big ones—in unexpected places. Nobody wants to sit still in the same place at such a big party. There will be more fidgeting than usual, I'm afraid. And first you must offer them all the best things you have. Later on it's all the same what they get because they'll be enjoying themselves anyway. And don't disturb them with songs, and so on—let them make the program themselves."

When the Muskrat had produced this surprising piece of worldly wisdom he retired to his hammock to read a book on "The Uselessness of Everything."

"What shall I wear?" the Snork Maiden asked Moomintroll, nervously. "The blue feather hair decoration or the pearl diadem?"

"Take the feathers," he said. "Just the feathers around your ears and ankles. And possibly two or three stuck into the tuft of your tail."

Thanking him she rushed away and collided in the doorway with the Snork, who was carrying some paper lanterns, and who muttered crossly about the uselessness of sisters, before he strode on into the garden and began hanging the lanterns in the trees.

Meanwhile the Hemulen was arranging firework set pieces in suitable places. They had Bengal Lights,

Blue-Star Rain, Silver Fountains, and Rockets that exploded with stars.

"This is so dreadfully exciting!" said the Hemulen. "Couldn't we let one off just to try?"

"It wouldn't be visible in the daylight," said Moominpappa. "But take a squib and let *that* off in the potato cellar if you like."

Moominpappa was busy on the verandah, making punch in a barrel. He put in almonds and raisins, lotus juice, ginger, sugar and nutmeg flowers, one or two lemons, and a couple of pints of strawberry liqueur to make it specially good.

Now and again he had a taste . . . It was *very* good.

"It's a pity about one thing," Sniff remarked. "We haven't any music—Snufkin isn't here."

"We'll use the wireless," said Moominpappa. "You'll see—everything will be all right—and we'll drink the second toast in Snufkin's honor."

"Whose is the first then?" asked Sniff, hopefully.

"Thingumy's and Bob's of course," said Moominpappa.

The preparations were getting more and more frenzied. The entire population of the valley, the woods, the hills, and the shore were coming with food and drink, which they spread out on the tables in the garden: there were big piles of gleaming fruit and huge plates of sandwiches on the bigger tables, and on tiny little tables under the bushes there were ears of corn and berries threaded on straws and clusters of nuts nestling in their own leaves. Moominmamma put the fat for frying the pancakes in the bathtub because there weren't enough basins, and then she carried up eleven enormous jars of raspberry juice from the cellar. (The twelfth had been cracked, I'm sorry to say, when the Hemulen let off his squib—but it didn't matter as Thingumy and Bob had licked most of it up.)

When it was dark enough to light the lanterns the Hemulen beat the gong as a signal for the party to begin.

Thingumy and Bob were sitting at the top of the biggest table. "Fancy!" they said. "So much buss and fother all in our honor! Can't understand it."

At first it was very solemn as everyone was dressed in his best, and felt a bit strange and uncomfortable. They greeted each other and bowed saying: "What a good thing it didn't rain and fancy the bag being found," and nobody dared to sit down.

Then Moominpappa made a little opening speech in which he began by explaining why the party was being held, and then thanked Thingumy and Bob, after which he made some remarks about the short August nights and how everyone should be as happy as possible, and then he began to talk about what it was like in his youth. This was the signal for Moominmamma to push in a whole trolleyful of pancakes, and everybody clapped.

Things at once began to liven up, and soon the party was in full swing. The whole garden—in fact the whole valley—was full of small lighted tables sparkling with fireflies and glowworms, and the lanterns in the trees swung to and fro like big shining fruit in the evening breeze.

The rockets leapt proudly up into the August sky, and exploded infinitely high up in a rain of white stars, which slowly sank down over the valley. All the little animals lifted their noses up to the starry rain and cheered—Oh, it was wonderful!

Then the Blue-star Rain began to fall and the Bengal Lights whirled over the treetops. And down the garden path came Moominpappa rolling the big barrel of red punch in front of him. Everybody came running down with their glasses, and Moominpappa filled every one—cups and bowls, birch bark mugs, shells, and even cornets made of leaves.

"Good health to Thingumy and Bob!" cried the whole of Moomin Valley. "Hip, Hip—Hurra! Hip, Hip—Hurra! Hip, Hip—Hurra!"

"Dappy hays!" said Thingumy to Bob, and they drank to each other's health.

Then Moomintroll got up on a chair and said, "Now I want to drink to the health of Snufkin, who is trekking south tonight all alone, but feeling I am sure as happy as we are here. Let us wish him a good pitch for his tent and a light heart!"

And on that everybody raised their glasses.

"You did speak well," said the Snork Maiden when Moomintroll sat down again.

"Oh, well . . ." he replied shyly, "of course I'd thought it all out beforehand."

Then Moominpappa carried the radio out into
the garden and tuned in to dance music from America,
and in no time the Valley was filled with dancing,
jumping, stamping, twisting, and turning. The trees

were thronged with dancing spirits, and even stiff-legged little mice ventured onto the dance floor.

Moomintroll bowed low to the Snork Maiden and said, "May I have the pleasure?" but as he looked up he caught sight of a shining light brimming over the treetops.

It was the August moon.

It sailed up, a deep orange color, unbelievably big and a little frayed round the edges like a tinned apricot, filling Moomin Valley with mysterious lights and shadows.

"Look! Tonight you can even see the craters on the moon," said the Snork Maiden.

"They must be awfully desolate," said Moomintroll. "Poor Hobgoblin up there hunting!"

"If we had a good telescope couldn't we see him?" asked the Snork Maiden. Moomintroll agreed but reminded her of their dance, and the party continued with more high spirits than ever.

"Are you tired?" asked Bob.

"No," said Thingumy. "I'm just thinking. Everyone has been so nice to us. We must try to roo something in deturn." And they whispered together for a while, nodded and whispered again. Then they went off to their secret hiding place and when they came out they were carrying the suitcase between them.

It was well after twelve o'clock when the whole valley was suddenly filled with a pinky-red light. Everybody stopped dancing as they thought it was a new firework, but it was only the opening of Thingumy and Bob's suitcase. The King's Ruby lay shining in the grass looking more beautiful than ever, making the fire, the lanterns and even the moon look pale and wan in comparison. Awestruck and speechless, they all crowded round the glowing jewel.

"To think that anything could be so beautiful!" exclaimed Moominmamma.

Sniff heaved a deep sigh and said, "Lucky Thingumy and Bob!"

But meanwhile the King's Ruby was shining like a red eye in the dark earth, and up in the moon the Hobgoblin caught sight of it. He had given up searching and sat tired and sad on the edge of a crater resting himself, while his black panther slept a little way off. He recognized the red point down on the earth at once—it was the biggest ruby in the world, the King's Ruby, which he had been hunting for for several hundred years! He started up and, with gleaming eyes, pulled on his gloves and fastened his cloak round his shoulders. He dropped all his other jewels to the ground—the Hobgoblin only troubled himself about one single precious stone, and that was the one he would hold in his hands in less than half an hour.

The panther threw himself into the air with his master on his back, and they began to hurtle through space—faster than light. Hissing meteors cut across their path and stardust caught in the Hobgoblin's cloak like driving snow, and it seemed to him that the red fire below burned more brightly. He steered

right toward the Valley of the Moomins, and with a
last spring the panther landed smoothly and silently
on the top of a Lonely Mountain.

The inhabitants of the Valley were still sitting in
silent awe in front of the King's Ruby. In its flame they
seemed to see all the wonderful things they had ever
done, and they longed to remember and to do them
once more. Moomintroll remembered his midnight rambles with Snufkin, and the Snork Maiden

thought of her proud conquest of the Wooden Queen. And Moominmamma imagined herself once more lying on the warm sand in the sunshine, looking up at the sky between the swaying heads of the sea-pinks.

Each one was far away, lost in wonderful memories, when they were all startled by a little white mouse with red eyes who slunk out of the wood and scurried towards the King's Ruby, followed by a coal-black cat which stretched itself out in the grass.

As far as anyone knew a white mouse had never lived in Moomin Valley, nor a black cat either.

"Puss! Puss!" said the Hemulen. But the cat only shut its eyes and didn't bother to answer.

Then the Wood-rat said, "Good evening, cousin!" but all she got from the white mouse was a long, melancholy stare. So Moominpappa came forward with two cups, wanting to offer the newcomers a drink from the barrel, but they took no notice of him.

A certain gloom crept over the Valley. People whispered and wondered. Thingumy and Bob got anxious and put the ruby back in their suitcase and shut the lid. But when they tried to take it away the white mouse stood up on his hind legs and began to grow. He grew almost as big as Moominhouse. He grew into the red-eyed Hobgoblin in white gloves, and when he had grown enough he sat down on the grass and looked at Thingumy and Bob.

"Go away you mugly old 'an!" said Thingumy.

"Where did you find the King's Ruby?" asked the Hobgoblin.

"Bind your own musiness!" said Bob.

They had never seen Thingumy and Bob being so brave.

"I have hunted for it for three hundred years," said the Hobgoblin. "I'm not interested in anything else."

"Nor are we," said Thingumy.

"You can't take it away from them," said Moomintroll. "They got it quite honestly from the Groke." (But he didn't mention how they had exchanged it for the Hobgoblin's own old hat—anyway he seemed to have a new one.)

"Give me something to munch," said the Hobgoblin. "This is getting on my nerves."

Moominmamma at once bustled forward with pancakes and jam, and gave him a big plateful.

While the Hobgoblin was eating they edged a little nearer. Somebody who eats pancakes and jam can't be so awfully dangerous. You can talk to him.

"Does it taste good?" asked Thingumy.

"Yes, thanks," said the Hobgoblin. "I haven't had a pancake for the last eighty-five years."

At once everybody felt sorry for him, and came still nearer.

When he had finished he wiped his moustache and said, "I can't take the ruby away from you, because that would be stealing. But couldn't you exchange it for, let's say, two diamond mountains and a valleyful of mixed precious stones?"

"No!" said Thingumy and Bob.

"And you can't give it to me?" asked the Hobgoblin.

"N-no . . ." they repeated.

The Hobgoblin sighed, and then he sat for a while thinking and looking very sad. At last he said:

"Well, go on with your party, and I'll cheer myself up by working a little magic for you. Everyone shall have a piece of magic for himself. Now you can all have a wish—the Moomin family first!"

Moominmamma hesitated a bit. "Should it be something you can see?" she asked. "Or an idea? If you know what I mean, Mr. Hobgoblin?"

"Oh, yes!" said the Hobgoblin. "Things are easier of course, but it will work with an idea too."

"Then I want to wish that Moomintroll will stop missing Snufkin," said Moominmamma.

"Oh, dear!" said Moomintroll going pink. "I didn't know it was so obvious!"

But the Hobgoblin waved his cloak once, and immediately the sadness flew out of Moomintroll's heart. His longing just became expectancy, and that felt much better.

"I've got an idea," he cried. "Dear Mr. Hobgoblin, make the whole table, with everything on it, fly away to Snufkin, wherever he is just now!"

At the same moment the table rose into the air and headed south with pancakes, jam, fruit and flowers, punch and sweets, and also the Muskrat's book which he had left on the corner.

"Hi!" said the Muskrat. "Now I should like my book spirited back again please."

"Right!" said the Hobgoblin. "Here you are, sir!"

"'On the Usefulness of Everything'," read the Muskrat. "But this is the wrong book. The one I had was about the Use*less*ness of Everything."

But the Hobgoblin only laughed.

"Surely it's my turn now," said Moominpappa, "but

it's very difficult to choose! I've thought of masses of things, but nothing is absolutely right. A greenhouse is more fun to make yourself; a dinghy, too. Besides I've got nearly everything."

"Perhaps you don't need a wish at all," said Sniff. "Couldn't I have yours?"

"Oh, well . . ." said Moominpappa, "I'm not sure about that . . ."

"You must hurry up, dear," urged Moominmamma. "What about wishing for a pair of really nice bookbindings for your Memoirs?"

"Oh! That *is* a good idea!" Moominpappa exclaimed happily, and everybody screamed with delight when the Hobgoblin handed over two red morocco-leather and gold bindings set with pearls.

"Me now!" squeaked Sniff. "A boat of my very own, please! A boat like a shell, with purple sails and a jacaranda mast and rowlocks made of emeralds!"

"That was quite a wish," said the Hobgoblin, kindly, and waved his cloak.

They all held their breath, but the boat didn't appear.

"Didn't it work?" asked Sniff in disappointment.

"Indeed it did," said the Hobgoblin, "but of course I put it down on the beach. You'll find it there in the morning."

"*With* rowlocks made of emeralds?" asked Sniff.

"Certainly. Four of them and one in reserve," said the Hobgoblin. "Next one, please!"

"Hm," said the Hemulen, "to tell you the truth there

was a botanizing spade that I borrowed from the Snork that got broken. So I simply must have a new one."

And he curtsied* in a well-brought-up manner when the Hobgoblin produced the new spade.

"Don't you get tired of working magic?" asked the Snork Maiden.

"Not with these easy things," answered the Hobgoblin. "And what will *you* have, my dear young lady?"

"It's really very difficult," said the Snork Maiden. "May I whisper?"

When she had whispered, the Hobgoblin looked a little surprised and asked, "Are you sure you want that to happen?"

"Yes! Sure!" breathed the Snork Maiden.

"Well—all right, then!" said the Hobgoblin. "Here we go!"

The next moment a cry of surprise went up from the crowd. The Snork Maiden was unrecognizable.

"What *have* you done to yourself?" said Moomintroll, frantically.

"I wished for eyes like the Wooden Queen," said the Snork Maiden. "You thought she was beautiful, didn't you?"

"Yes—b-but . . ." said Moomintroll, unhappily.

"Don't you think my new eyes are beautiful?" said the Snork Maiden, and started to cry.

---

*The Hemulen always curtsies because it looks so silly to bow in a dress. *Author.*

"Well, well," said the Hobgoblin, "if they aren't right then your brother can wish for the old eyes back again, can't he?"

"Yes, but I'd thought of something quite different," protested the Snork. "If she makes stupid wishes, it really isn't my fault!"

"What had you thought of?" asked the Hobgoblin.

"A machine for finding things out," said the Snork, "a machine that tells you whether things are right or wrong, good or bad."

"That's too difficult," said the Hobgoblin, shaking his head, "I can't manage that."

"Well, in that case I should like a typewriter," said the Snork, sulkily. "My sister can see just as well with her new eyes!"

"Yes, but she doesn't look so nice," said the Hobgoblin.

"Dearest brother," cried the Snork Maiden, who

had gotten hold of a mirror. "Please wish my little old eyes back again! I look so awful!"

"Oh, all right!" said the Snork at last. "You shall have them for the sake of the family. But I hope you're a little less vain in future."

The Snork Maiden looked in the mirror again and cried with delight. Her funny little eyes were back in their place again, but her eyelashes had actually become a little longer. Beaming all over her face she hugged her brother and said: "Sweetie-pie! Honey-pot! You shall have a typewriter as a Christmas present from me!"

"Don't!" said the Snork, who was very embarrassed. "One shouldn't kiss when people are looking. No, I couldn't bear to see you in that awful state—that's all."

"Ah, ha! Now only Thingumy and Bob are left from the house party!" said the Hobgoblin. "You can have a joint wish, because I can't tell the difference between you."

"Aren't *you* going to wake a mish?" asked Bob.

"I can't," replied the Hobgoblin sadly, "I can only give other people wishes, and change myself into different things."

Thingumy and Bob stared at him. Then they put their heads together and whispered for a long time.

Then Bob said solemnly. "We've decided to wake a mish for you because you are nice. We want a booby as rootiful as ours."

Everybody had seen the Hobgoblin laugh, but

nobody believed he could smile. He was so happy that you could see it all over him—from his hat to his boots! Without a word he waved his cloak over the grass—and behold! Once more the garden was filled with a pink light and there on the grass before them lay a twin to the King's Ruby—the Queen's Ruby.

"Now you're mot niserable anymore?" said Bob.

"I should say not," said the Hobgoblin, tenderly lifting up the shining jewel in his cloak. "And now every single one of the animals shall wish for what he wants! I shall grant all your wishes before morning, because I have to be home before the sun rises!"

And now they all had their turn.

In front of the Hobgoblin there circled a long line of chirping, laughing, humming forest creatures, who all wanted to have their wishes granted. Those who wished stupidly were allowed another chance, because the Hobgoblin was in a very good temper. The dancing started again, and more trolleyfuls of pancakes were wheeled under the trees. The Hemulen let off more and more fireworks, and Moominpappa carried out his Memoirs in their smart new binding and read aloud about his youth.

Never had there been such a celebration in the Valley of the Moomins.

Oh, what a wonderful feeling when you have eaten up everything, drunk everything, talked of everything, and danced your feet off, to go home in the quiet hour before the dawn to sleep!

And now the Hobgoblin flies to the end of the world and the Mother Mouse creeps into her nest, and one is as happy as the other.

But perhaps the happiest of all is Moomintroll, who goes home through the garden with his mother, just as the moon is fading in the dawn, and the trees rustling in the morning breeze which comes up from the sea.

It is autumn in Moomin Valley, for how else can spring come back again?

Tove Jansson
and the
Moomins

Tove Jansson was born in August 1914 and grew up in Helsinki. Her family, part of the Swedish-speaking minority of Finland, was artistic and eccentric. Tove's father, Viktor, was one of Finland's great sculptors, and her mother, Signe, designed and illustrated books and book jackets, postage stamps, banknotes, and political cartoons. The family kept a pet monkey named Poppolino, whom they dressed in argyle sweaters, and their house was often filled with visiting artists and other colorful guests.

As a young woman, Tove studied art and design in Sweden, Finland, and France, and chose to return to Finland to live. In the 1940s, she worked as an illustrator and cartoonist for various national magazines. During this time, she began using a Moomin-like figure as a kind of signature device in her cartoons. Called Snork, this early version of Moomintroll was thin, with a long, narrow nose and a devilish tail. Tove said that she had designed him in her youth, trying to draw "the ugliest creature imaginable."

The name "Moomintroll" began as a family joke: when Tove was studying in Stockholm and living with her Swedish relations, her uncle tried to stop her from pilfering food by telling her that a "Moomintroll" lived in the kitchen pantry and breathed cold air down people's necks.

Tove published the first Moomin book, *The Moomins*

and the Great Flood, in 1945, although it had been written as early as 1939. Sadly, it was not a success, perhaps in part because the Moomins in this earliest book looked like their Snork forebears: taller, less plump, and prone to anxious expressions. While the central characters are Moominmamma and Moomintroll, most of the principal characters of later stories were only introduced in the next book, so *The Moomins and the Great Flood* is frequently considered a "prequel" to the main series.

Acclaim arrived with the publication of *Comet in Moominland* in 1946 and *Finn Family Moomintroll* two years later. The books were soon published in English and other languages, and so began the Moomins' international rise to fame. Originally written in Swedish, the eight main books in the series have been translated into over thirty languages, including Icelandic, Persian, Ukrainian, and Welsh.

According to the author, "It all started with my wanting to depict an unusually happy family: they are all fond of each other and give each other all the freedom they need; it is a harmonious family. I think I have probably been thinking of my own childhood, which was a very happy one . . . As I went on writing and telling stories, the family grew, made friends and acquaintances, and some enemies as well, and somehow everything developed spontaneously."

Tove Jansson died in June 2001. The many honors she received as an author and artist include the Hans Christian Andersen Medal, awarded in 1966 by the International Board on Books for Young People for her lifetime contribution to children's books, and two gold medals from the Swedish Academy.

The beloved creator of Moominvalley and all its inhabitants once claimed that persnickety Little My was one of her favorite Moomin characters. "She's been very useful to me . . . She corrects the balance when things begin to get too emotional by chipping in with her sharp, cynical remarks. I think these Moomintrolls *are* so terribly emotional."

A Timeline Full of Fun Facts
About the World of Moomin

1914 Tove Jansson is born in Helsinki, Finland.

1945 The first Moomin story—*The Moomins and the Great Flood*—is published.

1946 The first full-length Moomin book—*Comet in Moominland*—is published.

1949 A theatrical version of *Comet in Moominland* is performed in the city of Turku in Finland.

1954 The world's largest newspaper, London's *Evening Standard*, starts running the Moomin comic strip. It continues until 1974, reaching 20 million readers daily in over 40 countries. Also, the first Moomin products come onto the market.

1959 The first Moomin television series—created with puppets—is aired in Germany.

1966 Tove Jansson wins the Hans Christian Award for her contribution to children's literature.

1969 A thirteen-part series called *Moomintroll* is produced in Sweden. An animated Moomin series in Japan also premieres and the international popularity of the Moomins grows.

1970 The last Moomin story—*Moominvalley in November*—is published. Tove decides to stop writing about the Moomins but continues to write for adults.

1974 The Moomin Opera opens in Helsinki.

1987 Moominvalley opens at the Tampere Art Museum. Tove Jansson's original Moomin works are part of a display containing 2,000 pieces of art. It also includes a blue five-story model of Moominhouse, built by Tove Jansson and others.

1989 Farrar Straus Giroux begins re-publishing the Moomin books in North America.

1990 Telecable produces a 104-part animated series about the Moomins. The series is sold to more than 60 countries.

1993 The theme park Moominworld opens in Naantali, Finland, and becomes a favorite European travel destination.

1990s Finnair paints Moomin characters on their airplanes.

2001 Tove Jansson dies.

2003 The *Moomin Voices* CD is released. Composed by Tove Jansson and Erna Tauro, it is a collection of Moomin songs which were first introduced to theater audiences in the 1950s.

2004 The Moomins and Tove Jansson are featured on a commemorative Finnish coin; one side depicts the artist and the other has three Moomin characters.

2006 Drawn and Quarterly begins to publish the original Moomin comic strips in English.

2010 marks the 65th anniversary of the Moomins!

Read all of the Moomin books

Comet in Moominland

When Moomintroll learns that a comet will be passing by, he and his friend Sniff travel to the Observatory on the Lonely Mountains to consult the Professors. Along the way, they have many adventures, encountering crocodiles, treasure, and more. But the greatest adventure of all awaits them when they learn that the comet is headed straight for their beloved Moominvalley.

Square Fish paperback
978-0-312-60888-0, $6.99 US/$8.50 Can
Farrar Straus Giroux hardcover
978-0-374-35030-7, $16.99 US/$19.95 Can

Finn Family Moomintroll

It is spring in the Valley of the Moomins, and Moomintroll and his friends make an exciting discovery: a shiny top hat with magical powers. When it's used as a wastepaper basket, it produces soft little clouds that everybody can ride. And when Moomintroll wears the hat, he turns into something he's not! But there is no knowing what the hat will do next and the magic may just be more trouble than it's worth.

Square Fish paperback
978-0-312-60889-7, $6.99 US/$8.50 Can
Farrar Straus Giroux hardcover
978-0-374-35031-4, $16.99 US/$19.95 Can

Moominpappa's Memoirs

As he recuperates from a bad cold, Moominpappa discovers it's the perfect time to ponder the Experiences that have made him the remarkable Moomin he is. Chapter by chapter, Moominpappa reads his memoirs to Moomintroll, Snufkin, and Sniff, and they learn of his triumphs, his tribulations, and his momentous meetings with the Joxter and the Muddler, the Mymble, and others too incredible to mention here.

Square Fish paperback
978-0-312-62543-6, $6.99 US/$8.50 Can
Farrar Straus Giroux hardcover
978-0-374-35035-2, $16.99 US/$19.95 Can

Moominsummer Madness

After being flooded out of their home, the resilient Moomins and their friends move into the first house that comes bobbing along. It's strange-looking, like a big cave with curtains hanging on either side. And when the house bumps into dry land and Moomintroll and the Snork Maiden decide to spend the night on shore—then the excitement really begins.

Square Fish paperback
978-0-312-60891-0, $6.99 US/$8.50 Can
Farrar Straus Giroux hardcover
978-0-374-35033-8, $16.99 US/$19.95 Can

Moominland Midwinter

Everyone knows that the Moomins sleep through the winter, but this year Moomintroll has woken up in January. After his initial shock at seeing his familiar haunts under the snow, Moomintroll discovers that winter is worth waking up for after all. In fact, more creatures than he ever imagined inhabit this new world, including a wise newcomer named Tooticky who introduces him to this most mysterious of all seasons.

Square Fish paperback
978-0-312-62541-2, $6.99 US/$8.50 Can
Farrar Straus Giroux hardcover
978-0-374-35034-5, $16.99 US/$19.95 Can

Tales from Moominvalley

Here are nine delightfully funny stories about the triumphs and tribulations of the citizens of Moominvalley. Readers will discover how the Moomin family save young Ninny from permanent invisibility, and what happens when Moomintroll catches the last dragon in the world. Some of the characters in these tales will be brand-new to Moomin fans, but there are lots of old friends to meet as well.

Square Fish paperback
978-0-312-62542-9, $6.99 US/$8.50 Can
Farrar Straus Giroux hardcover
978-0-374-35042-0, $16.99 US/$19.95 Can

Moominpappa at Sea

Leave Moominvalley? Is it possible? Yes, even the Moomin family need a change of scenery sometimes, so they're off to live in a lighthouse on a tiny island. Here they find space to grow, and to do things they couldn't in their comfortable, cluttered Valley home. As they discover their new home, the family also discover surprising, and wonderfully funny, new things about themselves.

Square Fish paperback
978-0-312-60892-7, $6.99 US/$8.50 Can
Farrar Straus Giroux hardcover
978-0-374-35032-1, $16.99 US/$19.95 Can

Moominvalley in November

Now that autumn is turning into winter, a group of unlikely friends—including the Fillyjonk, the Hemulen, and Toft—are waiting in Moominvalley to see the Moomins, for winter doesn't seem right without them. But the Moomins are not at home. So all the visitors settle down to await their return, and oddly enough find themselves warming up to their new life together. For Moominvalley is Moominvalley still, even without the Moomins in it.

Square Fish paperback
978-0-312-62544-3, $6.99 US/$8.50 Can
Farrar Straus Giroux hardcover
978-0-374-35036-9, $16.99 US/$19.95 Can